INTO THE DARK

Peter Abrahams, described by Stephen King as his "favourite suspense novelist", is a bestselling author of adult crime thrillers. His novels include *A Perfect Crime*; *The Fan*, which was adapted into a major Hollywood movie starring Robert De Niro; and *Lights Out*, which was nominated for an Edgar Award for best novel. The first title in the Echo Falls trilogy, *Down the Rabbit Hole* – so-called because it features the play *Alice's Adventures in Wonderland* – was a *New York Times* bestseller and won the Agatha Award for Best Young Adult Mystery; it is now followed by *Behind the Curtain* and *Into the Dark*. Peter lives in Cape Cod, Massachusetts, USA, with his wife and children.

INTO THE DARK

An Echo Falls Mystery

PETER ABRAHAMS

**WALKER
BOOKS**

Published by arrangement with HarperCollins Children's Books,
a division of HarperCollins, Inc.

First published in Great Britain 2008 by Walker Books Ltd
87 Vauxhall Walk, London SE11 5HJ

2 4 6 8 10 9 7 5 3 1

© 2008 Pas de Deux

This book has been typeset in Sabon

Printed in and bound in Great Britain by Clays Ltd, St Ives plc

British Library Cataloguing in Publication Data:
a catalogue record for this book is available from the British Library

ISBN 978-1-4063-0030-7

www.walkerbooks.co.uk

For school librarians everywhere

one

"brucie?" said Jill Monteiro, director of the Prescott Players. "Could we have that line again?"

"'Do not vorry, my little Gretel,'" Brucie said. "'All vill be vell.'"

Jill gazed at him for a moment, her dark eyes thoughtful. "Ah," she said. "That would be a German accent?"

"Jawohl, Kommandant," said Brucie.

"Hansel being German," Jill said.

Brucie clicked his heels.

"Interesting," said Jill.

"Oh, dear," said Sylvia Breen, cast as the witch but in real life assistant head teller at Central State Savings and Loan. "I'm no good at accents. No good at all."

"You see the problem, Brucie," Jill said.

"Nein," said Brucie.

"Either everybody does a German accent or nobody," she said.

"Completely hopeless," said Mrs. Breen.

"So we're gonna take a vote?" Brucie said.

Ingrid Levin-Hill, sitting on a stool beside Mrs. Breen, script in her hand and all Gretel's lines underlined in red, saw that Brucie's right leg was doing that twitchy thing. Ingrid loved being in the Prescott Players, loved this beautiful little theater in Prescott Hall, loved everything about putting on plays – especially working with Jill. Jill was a real actress: she'd been in a Hollywood movie, *Tongue and Groove*, where she'd said, "Make it a double," to the Eugene Levy character with this wicked look in her eye; best moment in the movie, in Ingrid's opinion. She'd watched the video many times – the only way anyone had ever seen the movie, since there'd been no actual theatrical release. Working with Jill was a privilege.

But working with Brucie? Ingrid had known Brucie most of her life. They had the very same birthday, a disturbing fact. She remembered Brucie on the playground, one of those kids – the only one, in her experience – who never tired of making himself dizzy. Now Brucie was the eighth-grade class clown at Ferrand Middle, taken seriously by no one. Until recently: about a month before, in fact, when his Xmas Revue performance of the wizard, in the scene where Oz is revealed to be a fraud, brought down the house – even though it wasn't supposed to be funny, and in rehearsal Brucie had missed every cue and botched his lines. But something had happened in the live performance, something that had prompted Mr. Samuels, editor and publisher of the Echo Falls *Echo*, to write in his "Arts, Entertainment, and Things to Do" column: "Do not miss the hilarious youngster Bruce Berman as the wizard like you've never seen him." Brucie carried the clipping in his pocket.

"I make a motion," he said, "zat ve do German accents."

The cast – Ingrid; Mrs. Breen; Meredith O'Malley (playing the woodcutter's wife), who looked a bit like Marilyn Monroe if Marilyn had reached middle age and let herself go; and the woodcutter, Mr. Santos, of Santos Texaco, who did a great wiseguy voice – all waited for Jill's reaction.

"Who vill second ze motion?" said Brucie.

Jill turned to him. "Know what I'm afraid of, Brucie?" she said.

"Grizzly bears?" said Brucie.

Jill blinked, a single blink, long and slow. Ingrid had never seen her do that before; for just a second, Jill didn't seem to be enjoying herself. "I'm afraid," she said, "of any additional little touch that might tip us into parody."

"Huh?" said Brucie.

"Parody," said Jill. "Like *Monty Python and the Holy Grail*."

"Monty Python?" said Brucie. "Three thumbs up." He got off his stool, pranced around the stage, making clip-clop sounds and banging imaginary coconuts together. "Python rules." Ingrid's best friend, Stacy, would have smacked him; Ingrid herself came close.

"Siddown," said Mr. Santos.

Brucie skidded to a stop and sat.

"Decisions like this always come back to understanding what the story is about," said Jill.

Silence.

"These two kids get kicked out of the house," said Mr. Santos.

"And meet up with a witch who lures them with a gingerbread house," said Meredith O'Malley.

"Don't forget the bread crumbs," said Mrs. Breen.

"You're giving me the plot," Jill said. "But what's it about? That's the root of everything we're going to do with this play." Jill was back to normal. She had a lovely, expressive face; even under the dim houselights it was shining.

"Kids on their own," Ingrid said.

Jill nodded. "Kids on their own," she said. "Yes – and deep in a dark and dangerous place."

"Ooo," said Meredith, in her breathy voice. "I just got a shiver."

"So – vote or no vote?" said Brucie.

Ingrid stood alone outside Prescott Hall – a huge old mansion with lots of towers and gargoyles, now mostly hidden by scaffolding. She waited for her ride. Nothing unusual about that: Mom and Dad had busy lives, were often late. Meanwhile a gray squirrel was running through the snow, a fast squirrel that kicked up tiny white puffs. Hey – it didn't really run, more like bounded along, the hind paws landing first. How come she'd never noticed that before? Like Sherlock Holmes, her favorite fictional character by far, Ingrid made a habit of observing small details. She took a close look at its tracks. Most were blurred because of how fast it had been going, but she found one clear set – the hind paws, landing first, had five toes; the front paws, actually landing behind, only four. People had the same number of fingers and toes, so why would—

Beep.

She turned, saw Dad's TT parked in the circular drive behind her. The window slid down. "Ingrid," Dad called, "I honked three times."

Ingrid got in the car. It smelled of Dad's aftershave – a nice smell.

"You really didn't hear me?" he said.

"Sorry, Dad."

"Got your head in the clouds these days," he said.

And you've been crabby for months. But Ingrid didn't say it. Dad worked hard – he was vice president at the Ferrand Group, and Ingrid was starting to understand that Mr. Ferrand was a pretty demanding boss. In good light now, on days like this, for example, she could see tiny lines at the corners of Dad's eyes; but still the handsomest dad in Echo Falls.

"How was rehearsal?" he said.

"Okay."

"What is it again?"

"*Hansel and Gretel.*"

"You're Gretel?"

"Yeah."

Dad nodded, drove down the long lane lined with old-fashioned lampposts. "Look in the glove compartment," he said, turning onto the highway.

Ingrid looked in the glove compartment. "For me?" she said.

"Open it," said Dad.

A present? Very small, but still … it wasn't her birthday or Christmas, and besides, Mom bought all the presents. She glanced at Dad. He was watching the road, poker-faced. Ingrid removed the wrapping – silver paper with a gold bow – and folded it carefully, just the way Mom did, although the saved old wrapping paper never seemed to get reused and ended up in the trash anyway. Inside was a tiny box; inside that, nestled in cotton, lay a ring. Ingrid had never seen one like it.

"That's a compass on top?" she said.

"So you always know the directions," Dad said. "They were selling them in the pro shop. I got the last one."

"Oh," said Ingrid. "Thanks." It was a big ring, too loose for anything but her middle finger. She slid it on. The red needle quivered and pointed toward E. "We're going east?"

Dad shook his head. "The needle always points north," he said. "Magnetic north. You know the whole planet's a big magnet, right?" First she'd heard of it, but Ingrid just nodded. Dad wasn't like this very often, explaining things – things that didn't have to do with sports, anyway. "Just shift your hand and it'll line up."

She shifted her hand. "North?"

"North to Grampy's," said Dad.

"Grampy's?"

"He wants some help stacking wood. Didn't Mom tell you?"

"What about Ty?" Ty was her fifteen-year-old brother, bigger and stronger, much better suited to stacking wood.

"He's studying for a science test."

Impossible. "It's Saturday, Dad."

"Ty's starting to take his schoolwork more seriously," Dad said.

"He is?" Were video games in the curriculum?

"In the nick of time," Dad said.

"Huh?"

"Ninth-grade results go on the college apps, Ingrid, become part of your permanent record," Dad said. "This is your last year for getting off scot-free."

"I plan to go crazy," Ingrid said.

He gave her a sharp look. She gave him back a poker face of her own. *College apps:* a hideous expression. And *permanent record* was pretty bad too. Ingrid never wanted to hear either of them again.

Dad drove up 392. At first the river ran toward their right – fast and black, narrowed by ice shelves creeping out from both banks – and the car headed straight toward N on the compass. Then 392 curved left, the river disappeared, and their route swung around toward W. Soon after that, Grampy's farm – the last farm left inside the boundaries of Echo Falls – appeared on the right: fields snowy, trees bare in the apple orchard, and the sheds, barn, house, their red paint long faded to a rusty brown.

"Dad?" she said as they parked in front of the house.

"Yeah?"

"Grampy said we stole the farm from the Indians. He was joking, right?"

They got out of the car. Ingrid could see her breath. It just hung in the still air. Wood-chopping sounds, thunking and splintering, came from the back of the house.

"Grampy's got his own sense of humor," Dad said.

"So it's not true?"

They walked around the house. Grampy came into view. He stood by the chopping block, his thick hair the exact same white as the fresh snow, ax held high and split logs all around. The ax flashed down. *Thwack* – and two more semi-cylinders of wood went flying.

"Hi, Dad," said Dad; always a weird moment for Ingrid, when Dad called Grampy that.

Grampy, placing another log on the block, turned; his nose was running. "Mark," he said. And to Ingrid, "Hi, kid."

"Hi, Grampy."

"Where's your jacket?" Dad said.

Grampy wore a flannel shirt, sleeves rolled up, and old corduroys, torn at the knees. Even though he was almost seventy-nine, ropes of muscle stood out in his forearms. "It's not cold," he said.

"I brought you some papers to sign," said Dad.

"What kind of papers?"

"Just some minutes, but the accountant's agitating for them." Dad took a manila envelope from an inside pocket of his suede coat.

"Leave them with Ingrid," said Grampy.

Dad handed the envelope to Ingrid, giving her a look that said, *Make sure he signs*. He buttoned his coat and walked back to the car.

*   *   *

"What are minutes, Grampy?"

"Paperwork," said Grampy. "Had it up to here with paperwork."

He chopped. Ingrid stacked, making nice even rows, each layer crosswise to the layer underneath, the way Grampy liked. The rows grew higher and higher. They didn't talk. *Thwack thwack thwack*. Ingrid sensed he was in a bad mood, could feel it, like weather. Sweat started dripping off his chin.

"How about a break?" Ingrid said.

Grampy paused. "Getting tired?"

"A little," Ingrid said. "Aren't you?"

"Nope."

"Not even your arms?"

"Arms got nothing to do with it," Grampy said. "Chopping wood's all about legs."

"It is?"

"Arms just take care of the finishing touch, hog all the glory," said Grampy. "C'mere." He stood a log on the block, gave Ingrid the ax. The edge of the blade gleamed. "Hands like this," he said, "and feet like so. Eyes on an imaginary vertical line right down the middle of that circle."

"Like watching the soccer ball?" Ingrid said. She hadn't played in weeks, was already starting to look forward to spring soccer.

"Yup. Now bend your knees, up with the blade, and swing it forward from the backs of your legs, little wrist snap at the end. And don't forget your toes."

"You mean not hit them, Grampy?"

"Why would you do a thing like that?" said Grampy.

"I mean curling them at the right moment."

Sounded odd, but Ingrid did what Grampy said, felt strength flowing up through her body from her legs, even curled her toes at what she thought might be the right moment. The blade came down, little wrist snap, and – *crack*. The log split in two, so smoothly her hands felt nothing, as though she'd been chopping a loaf of bread.

"Hey!"

"Now you can be a lumberjack when you grow up," Grampy said, in a better mood now; she could hear it in his voice. "How about a cup of something hot?"

They went in the back, Grampy carrying an armful of firewood, Ingrid holding the door. The phone was ringing. Grampy, busy at the wood box, ignored it; typical Grampy. It rang and rang. No answering machine picked up because Grampy didn't have an answering machine.

"Grampy? It might be Mom or Dad."

"Answer it then," Grampy said, piling wood in the fireplace.

Ingrid picked up the phone. "Hello?"

A man, but not Dad. "Aylmer Hill, please," he said. "This is Dr. Pillman."

"For you," Ingrid said.

Grampy took the phone. He listened for a moment, said, "Wrong number," and hung up.

two

they sat at the table in Grampy's kitchen. A fire burned in the huge fireplace, a roaring ten-log fire. Ingrid brewed tea. Grampy poured a little VO into his. He opened a can of peanuts. Ingrid slid the manila envelope toward him. Grampy, busy eating peanuts, didn't seem to notice.

"About the Indians," Ingrid said.

"Indians?" Grampy looked up; he had bluish patches under both eyes, like bruises.

"The ones you said we stole the farm from."

"What about them?"

"Is it true?"

Grampy gazed at her; he had clear blue eyes, a wintry shade of blue like today's sky. "Got something to show you," he said. He rose, left the room; she heard his footsteps on the stairs, then creaking on the floorboards overhead.

Then silence. Ingrid drank her tea. She ate peanuts. She got up and poked at the fire. She checked the fridge, found some old lemons and three jars of peanut butter. She looked in the cupboard – peanuts, peanut brittle, a bag of marshmallows.

"Grampy?" she called. "Want me to roast some marshmallows?" No answer. "Grampy?" She left the kitchen, went to the foot of the stairs. "Grampy?"

Ingrid got a funny feeling in her stomach, like nervousness but a bit lower down. She climbed the stairs, dark wooden stairs, very old-looking, with a faded maroon carpet running down the middle. Had she ever actually been upstairs at the farm? Maybe once: that maroon runner triggered a memory, maybe her earliest. She knew, without even putting a hand on it, how this runner would feel to the touch. Was it possible she'd crawled up?

A shadowy corridor led to the right. There were three doors off it, but somehow Ingrid also knew the first one was Grampy's bedroom. The door was open. Ingrid looked in.

Grampy's bedroom was simple: dresser, bedside table, bed. He lay on it, eyes closed, fully clothed, boots still on; his red-and-black-checked lumber jacket hung on the bedpost. Ingrid watched until she was sure she wasn't imagining the up-and-down movement of his chest. His face was still; it looked much older asleep, really ancient.

It was cold upstairs. A blanket lay folded at the end of the bed, just beyond Grampy's feet. Ingrid went in quietly, unfolded the blanket, and laid it over Grampy. A framed photo of a dark-haired woman with features a lot like Dad's stood on the bedside table: Grampy's wife. And also Ingrid's grandmother, but she'd died many years ago, long before Ingrid's birth, before anyone could attach one of those grandparent names like Grammy or Grandma to her. She was standing on a balcony, or maybe a pier, waving and smiling. Ingrid backed out of the room.

She went downstairs, called home. Ty picked up.

"How's that homework going?" she said.

"Huh?" said Ty.

"Is Mom or Dad there?"

Ty shouted, "Mom! Dad!" Pause. "Guess not," he said.

"Where are they?"

"Do I look like a search engine?"

"That joke wasn't funny the first time. I need to be picked up."

"So?" said Ty. "What am I supposed to do?"

Downstairs Ingrid put her jacket on – a red jacket, red being her favorite color, the only one that said COLOR in big letters – and went out to the barn. Even just a few years ago lots of animals had lived on the farm, but now there was just one piglet – for tax purposes, Grampy said. He lived in a plywood pen she'd helped Grampy build, a pen kept in the barn for the winter. Ingrid unlatched the little door.

"Here, Piggy."

Piggy ran out, not even glancing at her, and headed straight for the shelf in the corner where Grampy kept the Slim Jims. He made snorting sounds.

"You're getting so big."

Piggy didn't care about that. He made more snorting sounds, kind of impatient now. Ingrid went over, peeled the wrapper from a Slim Jim, tore some off. Piggy tilted up his head, opened wide. Ingrid dropped the piece in. Gone in one chomp. More snorting, right away.

"Don't you even chew?"

Head up, mouth open. Ingrid could see the tail end of the Slim Jim, way at the back. She dropped in the rest. *Chomp. Snort.*

"That's it, Piggy. Back in your pen."

But Piggy didn't want to go back in the pen. A single Slim Jim still lay on the shelf, and his eyes – tiny but intelligent, even calculating, reminding her slightly of her math teacher, Ms. Groome – were locked on it. Ingrid reached into a bin for a handful of hay, covered up the Slim Jim.

"All gone," she said.

Piggy snorted and didn't budge. He wasn't buying it for a second. Was this what being a mother would be like? If so, forget it.

"You know you're only allowed one," Ingrid said. Grampy had a rule – although why it mattered, since pigs ate just about everything including slops and garbage and therefore couldn't be spoiled, was something she didn't under—

What was that? Voices? Yes, some commotion outside: angry voices. Ingrid went to a window, wiped away the grime. From there she could see the front of the house, about twenty or thirty yards away. A green van stood in the driveway, with stenciled words on the side: DEPARTMENT OF CONSERVATION. Grampy stood in the doorway of the house, facing a man about his own size, white-haired like Grampy but younger, dressed in a uniform, same color as the van. He had some papers in his hand and shook them at Grampy. Grampy batted them away with the back of his hand, scattering the papers in the snow. The man in green jumped back and snatched something from his pocket.

A camera?

Yes. The man in green stooped over and started taking close-ups of the scattered papers. That seemed to infuriate Grampy. He spun around and disappeared in the house. But not for long: A moment or two later he was back, the .22 rifle in his hands, barrel pointed to the ground. Ingrid banged open the barn door and raced outside.

"Grampy! Grampy!"

The men turned to her. They both froze for a moment. Then Grampy took the rifle and stuck it inside the house, out of sight. The man in green put his camera away and picked up the papers. Ingrid came to a halt a few steps away.

"What's happening?" she said. "What's wrong?"

The man in green – much younger than Grampy, one of those prematurely gray guys – turned back to Grampy and said, "I'm trying to do my lawful duty."

Grampy said, "This is my land. Get off."

The man in green folded the papers. "I'll be back," he said. "With a warrant and police protection if necessary."

Grampy started trembling. "I wouldn't do that if I were you," he said.

They glared at each other. Then the man in green got

in his van and drove away, spraying gravel. Ingrid went over to Grampy. She hated to see him trembling like that, but the look in his eye – so fierce – made the notion of hugging him or even touching his arm out of the question.

"Grampy?" she said. "What's going on?"

He turned to her, the look in his eye slowly fading, as though he was coming out of some sort of trance. He took a deep breath. "Total breakdown of society," he said.

"What's the Department of Conservation?"

"Meddlers," said Grampy.

"What do they want?"

"To make trouble."

"How? I don't understand."

He took another deep breath, stopped trembling. All at once his mood changed; he looked a lot better, those bruises under his eyes now almost gone. He smiled down at Ingrid. "Nothing to worry about, kid," he said. "All taken care of." He brushed his hands together, like after a job well done. "How about we roast up some marsh—"

A soft crashing sound came from the side of the house. Ingrid and Grampy went around to look. The pig had knocked over a trash can and disappeared inside, all except for his twisted tail, which twitched wildly. Oh God – she'd left the barn door open.

"Here, Piggy," Ingrid called.

The tail went still. Ingrid and Grampy walked through the snow, stood over the trash can.

"Come on out," Ingrid said.

The pig snorted and came barreling out of the trash can, backward but very quick.

"Grab 'im," said Grampy.

Ingrid reached for the pig, too late. He ran toward the orchard. Grampy said, "Weee-oooo," surprising Ingrid, and then surprised her more by taking off after it, maybe not fast, but actually running. That terrified the pig, no question. It swerved, changing directions. Ingrid ran to head it off. One thing about Ingrid: she could run. The snow, not too deep, hardly slowed her down at all. The pig heard her coming and tried to go faster, his little hooves flailing away in a cartoonish blur until he lost his balance and tumbled down. Ingrid fell on top of him, and so did Grampy, the three of them rolling over and over in the snow. When they came to a stop, the pig's face ended up side by side with Grampy's.

Grampy saw that and started laughing, a rich, wonderful laugh, almost the laugh of a young man. Tears rose in his eyes and ran down his face. A crazed look appeared in Piggy's eyes. He squealed, wriggled free, and raced across the field and straight into the barn, never looking back.

Ingrid sat up. "Grampy? Are you all right?"

He stopped laughing, wiped away the tears, and rose, not easily. She heard his knees crack. "You're a good kid," he said, and brushed some snow out from under the collar of her jacket.

"How was Grampy?" Mom said, driving Ingrid home in the MPV.

A tough question. "What's the Department of Conservation?" Ingrid said.

"The county agency that protects the environment," Mom said. "Why?"

"One of them came to see Grampy today."

"Oh," said Mom. Her eyes shifted toward Ingrid. Mom had big dark eyes that seemed to pull in all kinds of information from the visual world, like some sort of special magnets. "What about?"

"I didn't really hear," Ingrid said. "But they sounded pretty mad at each other." Ingrid left out the .22. Guns were – what was that word? anathema? – to Mom; no sense alarming her unnecessarily.

"What did the conservation agent look like?" Mom said.

"He had white hair like Grampy, but much younger."

"Oh, dear."

"You know him?"

"From work," Mom said. Mom was a real estate agent at Riverbend Properties, their third highest seller two years before; lately the market had cooled off, and Mom hadn't sold anything in months. "It sounds like Harris Thatcher. I wish they'd sent somebody else."

"Why?"

"Harris is a bit of a hothead."

"Yeah," said Ingrid.

"The kind of person who'd rub Grampy the wrong way," Mom added.

Ingrid nodded. "But he cheered up afterward. We roasted marshmallows."

"Does he still like them burned to a crisp?"

"Yup."

Mom smiled. She glanced over at Ingrid again. "What's that on your finger?"

"A compass ring," Ingrid said. She extended her hand so Mom could see. "I'll never get lost again." Following the example of Sherlock Holmes – who carried a detailed map of London in his head – Ingrid had been trying for months, not too successfully, to do the same with Echo Falls.

"Where did you get it?" Mom said.

"Dad gave it to me."

"He did?" Mom was beautiful. She had lovely soft skin, still unlined, except for when she was worried or puzzled about something. Then two deep vertical grooves would appear, right between her eyes, two grooves that were visible at that moment. "That was nice of him," Mom said.

three

"um."

"Hi, Joey."

"Hi." Ingrid could hear Joey's father, Echo Falls police chief Gilbert L. Strade, in the background saying, "Speak up. Don't mumble." Then came some bumping sounds, a door closing, and Joey again, his voice now clearer, silence in the background. "Hi," he said.

"Hi."

"I called yesterday."

"I was at my grandfather's."

"Yeah. Ty said." Silence. "Now you're back."

"Uh-huh."

"Back home."

"Right."

"Guess what."

"I give up."

"'Member what I got for Christmas?"

"Snowshoes?"

"I tried them out today. In those woods."

"The town woods?"

"Yeah." Silence.

"And?"

"And what?"

"You might like it."

"Like what?"

"Snowshoeing."

"I don't have snowshoes, Joey. You do."

"That's the thing." Long pause. "You know Play It Again?"

"The secondhand sports store?"

"I was in there the other day. Not yesterday but the day before." Long pause. "Anyways," said Joey.

"Anyways what?" said Ingrid.

"The thing is, they were in pretty good shape," Joey said.

"What were?"

"Pretty good shape for the price," Joey added. "Which I can't tell you on account of they're like sort of a present."

Ingrid, who'd been lounging on her bed with the cordless phone – not a cell phone, since she didn't have one, thirteen being considered too young for cell phones at 99 Maple Lane – sat up. "You got me a present?"

"It's no big deal," said Joey.

"What is it?"

"What is what?"

"The present, Joey."

"I already told you," said Joey. "Secondhand snowshoes."

"Oh," said Ingrid. "Thanks."

"Not too banged up," Joey said. "No warping or nothin'. And guess what?"

"What?"

"They're red."

"Yeah?"

"Your favorite color."

"Thanks, Joey."

"Hey," said Joey. "So how's right now?"

"Right now?"

"For trying them out," said Joey. "Don't you want to try them out?"

Ingrid was actually in the mood – and this often seemed to happen after spending time with Grampy – for taking it easy, maybe whipping up a batch of peanut butter squares, her own recipe featuring white chocolate chips, and memorizing some of Gretel's lines. "Outside?" she said.

"Unless you've got snow in your room," Joey said.

He'd cracked a joke. Did that ever happen? Ingrid couldn't think of a single example. And this was a funny joke, way funnier than any ever cracked by Brucie Berman, who'd once almost won a bet that he could keep up a rate of three jokes a minute for the entire school bus ride, and had been doing great until Mr. Sidney suddenly slammed on the brakes. Ingrid laughed and laughed.

"What?" said Joey. "What's so funny?"

One of the nicest things about 99 Maple Lane – and there were lots, even though it didn't come close to being the fanciest house in the Riverbend neighborhood

– was the fact that it backed right up to the town woods, acres and acres of undeveloped land that stretched all the way to the river. Now – a few days after a heavy snowfall – the woods were silent, except for the light swishing of Joey's snowshoes and the heavier thudding of Ingrid's as she fell farther and farther behind. Ingrid could run – would blow Joey away in any kind of footrace – but this was different, more of a plodding motion, sinking four or five inches into the puffy snow with every step. For some reason Joey could plod very fast. Ingrid plodded after him on snowshoes that weren't really what she would call red, more of a maroon, although Joey didn't realize that; he was already calling them her red sleds. Joke number two – not as funny.

He turned – a long way up the path, already way past the old tree house Dad had built for Ty and Ingrid when they were little – and said, "Cool, huh?"

"You'll have to shout," Ingrid said.

"Huh?"

Because you're so far ahead. But Ingrid left that unspoken. Instead she tried copying his stride, longer than hers, and viola! (as she'd heard Meredith O'Malley say more than once instead of *voilà*), thudding turned to swishing and her speed picked up. She began to feel more at home on the snowshoes, and at the same time more a part of the woods. The path, marked here and there by ski tracks, went up a long rise, the trees growing more closely together, dark and still. Breath clouds rose above Joey's head, hung in the air for a moment or two, then vanished. Ingrid caught up to him at the big rock – spray-painted with RED RAIDERS RULE! – where the Punch Bowl came in sight. His face was shining.

"They used to run traplines," he said.

"Huh?"

"The pioneers," Joey said. "In woods just like this."

"What's a trapline?"

"With bait," said Joey. "A muskrat steps into it, or maybe a deer, and…" He glanced to the side of the trail, saw some tracks, and pointed. "Bet that's muskrat right there," he said.

Ingrid went closer. She had only a vague idea of what a muskrat looked like, but she recognized these tracks: five-toed imprints in front, four-toed imprints behind. "Gray squirrel," she said.

Joey turned to her. "Yeah?"

Ingrid explained how she knew.

"Hey," Joey said. He took off his baseball cap – Echo Falls boys kept their ears uncovered no matter how cold the weather – and scratched his head, scratched hard, in a way that reminded her of her dog, Nigel. That stubborn cowlick, like a blunt Indian feather, stood straight up. He caught her looking at him, and the expression on his face changed. Joey took a step forward. His face seemed to get a little heavier. Was a kiss coming? Possibly, but Joey's next step banged down on the front of her right snowshoe, a surprisingly loud sound in the woods. He backed away, flailing a little for balance. After some awkward shuffling around – doubly awkward on snowshoes – they got back onto the trail.

"They ate squirrels, too," Joey said over his shoulder after a while. "The pioneers."

"We've come a long way," said Ingrid.

They started circling the Punch Bowl – an almost perfectly round pond formed by a glacier, although Ingrid could never keep the exact sequence of events in order.

"Were the Indians here when it was a glacier?" she said.

"Maybe," said Joey. "Wanna cut across?"

The Punch Bowl was frozen over, the ice covered in snow in some places, bare in others where the wind had scoured it. Ingrid saw some ski tracks out there, and scraps of black hockey-stick tape.

"At least a foot thick this year," Joey said. "The ice. My dad says."

They cut across the Punch Bowl. Once or twice Ingrid heard cracking, like ice cubes when soda first hits them, but deeper.

"Just compression," Joey said.

"What's that?" said Ingrid.

"You know," said Joey. "Kind of like…"

They climbed the far bank and picked up the trail. Glancing back, Ingrid saw they'd saved maybe a minute. But she trusted Chief Strade.

"Joey?"

"Yeah?" *Swish swish:* Around another bend and out of sight he went, this time leaving a breath cloud that lingered in the air without him.

"Ever see *Doctor Zhivago*?"

His voice drifted back through the trees. "What's that?"

"A movie."

"What about?"

"An endless trudge through frozen wastes."

"Endless what through what?"

Ingrid rounded the bend. Joey was waiting at a fork in the trail. A cross-country skier had taken the right fork; to the left the snow lay smooth and unbroken.

"Ever been this far?" Joey said.

"No."

"Me neither. But I think one of these comes out near the falls."

"Yeah?" Ingrid said.

"Didn't Mr. Porterhouse say something about it?"

Mr. Porterhouse was the gym and health teacher at Ferrand Middle. Just about anything came up in his class, a whole stream of tidbits flowing by, few snagging in Ingrid's mind.

Joey's nose was running, two tiny streams, clear and shiny. "But which one?" he said.

Ingrid took off her mitten.

"What's that?" Joey said, coming closer.

"Compass ring," Ingrid said, at that moment realizing she'd received two presents, compass ring and snowshoes; kind of a red-letter weekend.

"Hey," said Joey.

"The river's west, right?" Ingrid said.

Joey gazed up at the sky, flat gray through the network of dark branches. "If the sun was out..." he began. Ingrid checked the compass ring and pointed to the unbroken path.

The path led up and up: much harder going now, the two of them making first tracks, huffing and puffing. First Joey was in the lead, but all at once Ingrid got her second wind – a great feeling of energy flowing through her, actually making her stronger and fresher than before they'd even started, her breathing back to normal, and she surged ahead, Joey glancing sideways in surprise.

They went around two sharp bends, came to a huge evergreen of the Christmas tree type. Spruce? Pine? Snow lay thick on all the branches. Ingrid felt a faint breeze on her face. Joey started to say something. She held up her hand. They listened. A sound came through the trees.

Shhh.

The sound of the falls, very faint. Ingrid almost said "Pioneers rule" but stopped herself. Talk like that might spoil things, this sensation that had been growing in her, of going back in time.

The trail took them past another tree, almost as big, then sloped down. After a minute or two they stepped into a clearing, and viola! The falls came suddenly into view, a few hundred yards away. The clearing stood level with the top of the falls, so they could see the river, frozen over upstream, black and roiling near the drop, and then the whole slow-motion creamy deluge into the wild whirlpools down below. And the best part: this was one of those spots where you could hear the strange double echo that had inspired the name Echo Falls, like a big loud voice shushing a small stubborn one that kept shushing it right back.

So much to look at: Ingrid didn't notice right away that there were two people in the picnic area down on the near bank, a popular spot in summer but not now.

They sat on a bench near the safety railing, huddled close together, perhaps a man and a woman, too far away to tell. Ingrid and Joey crossed the clearing, back into the woods, following the path down switchbacks, the double *shhh* growing louder. It rose almost to a roar as they walked through the last trees and into the picnic area; like Lewis and Clark, Ingrid thought.

There was only one person on the bench now, a woman in a long black coat, pretty fashionable for a winter visit to the falls. As Ingrid and Joey moved toward the railing, she turned to them. Her eyes were red – from crying? Were those tears on her cheeks? And then Ingrid realized who it was.

"Mrs. McGreevy?" she said.

Mrs. McGreevy, mother of Mia, one of Ingrid's best friends, looked startled. Her face paled, going almost as white as the snow. "Ingrid?" she said.

"Yeah," said Ingrid. "Hi."

"Hi," Mrs. McGreevy said, her hand, for a moment, covering her heart. "I…" She gestured at the falls. "I was taking a look. In winter, I mean. It's so … so beautiful. Beautiful and scary."

"Yeah," said Ingrid. Beautiful and scary: Mom had said the exact same thing, more than once.

Mrs. McGreevy's gaze went from Ingrid to Joey, back to Ingrid. She licked her lips. "Mia's at the library," she said. She and Mia had moved to Echo Falls from New York the year before, after Mrs. McGreevy's divorce.

"At the library?" Ingrid said.

"Working on a paper," said Mrs. McGreevy. "The Whiskey Rebellion? Something like that."

Uh-oh. Whiskey Rebellion – when was that due?

"In fact," said Mrs. McGreevy, "I should probably go pick her up." She glanced at her car, a green hatchback; from here you could see the parking lot and the entrance to River Road, invisible from the clearing above. "Can I give you kids a ride?" She took out her keys, dropped them, picked them up.

"We're on snowshoes," Joey said.

Mrs. McGreevy blinked, as though he'd spoken in a foreign language.

"This is Joey," Ingrid said. "Mrs. McGreevy."

"Hello."

"Um. Hi."

"Well, then." Mrs. McGreevy started moving away. "I'll be going. Nice running into – nice seeing you." She walked to the parking lot, got into her car – the only one in the lot – and drove off.

"What's with her?" Joey said. "Like she never heard of snowshoes?"

"She's a city person," Ingrid said.

"Yeah," said Joey. "But still."

The falls went *shhh shhh*.

the history teacher didn't show up Wednesday morning, which meant, one: a sub, in this case Mr. Porterhouse, gym and health teacher, and two: an automatic extension on the Whiskey Rebellion paper, a lucky break for Ingrid, who'd forgotten all about it once, remembered in the picnic area at the falls, and then somehow forgotten again.

"What," said Mr. Porterhouse, reading from a note card, "is the significance of the Boston Tea Party?"

No hands went up.

"C'mon, you sports," said Mr. Porterhouse; he called everyone "sport." "The Boston Tea Party – dawn's early light, rockets' red glare, big big big."

Ingrid, who thought she'd had a pretty good grip on the Boston Tea Party until that moment, now wasn't sure.

Still no hands. Mr. Porterhouse fingered the whistle that always hung around his neck. Was he going to blow it? "Know what they say about them that – those that forget history?"

No hands.

"They're totally—" Mr. Porterhouse stopped whatever he was going to say, backed up. "They're in the cra— in the toilet, is what." He paused to let that sink in. "So, Boston Tea Party, significance of."

Brucie raised his hand. Mr. Porterhouse didn't see him. Brucie waved his hand around like a red-carpet celebrity. He was invisible to Mr. Porterhouse.

"'Kay," said Mr. Porterhouse. "Baby steps. Where did it happen?"

Where did the Boston Tea Party happen? Was that what he was asking? Ingrid sat up; this was starting to get interesting.

Mr. Porterhouse suddenly whirled and pointed straight at Dustin Dratch, sitting beside his twin brother, Dwayne; easy to tell them apart – Dustin had the cauliflower ear. They were the biggest kids at Ferrand Middle by far, partly because they were fifteen, having been held back twice despite the social promotion rule in Echo Falls schools.

"Tell the people, Dustin," said Mr. Porterhouse.

"What people?" asked Dustin.

Dwayne made a snorting noise, its meaning unclear.

"These people, Dustin," said Mr. Porterhouse. "Your fellow scholars."

Dustin looked around the room, squinting a bit, as though trying to spot something cleverly hidden. "Tell 'em what, again?" he said.

"Whereabouts of the Boston Tea Party," said Mr. Porterhouse.

From where Ingrid sat, she could see Dwayne nudge Dustin under desk level, and maybe whisper something quickly too, although they might have just relied on twin telepathy. Whatever the message, Dustin passed it on to the class. "They had it in a restaurant," he said. "Like, where else?"

"Think they'll be held back again?" said Mia at recess. They sat on the swings in the farthest corner of the yard at Ferrand Middle, not swinging, just dangling in the cold: Ingrid, Ingrid's best friend, Stacy Rubino, and Mia.

"No way," Stacy said. "Next year they'll be sixteen. You can drop out of school at sixteen."

"Yeah?" said Ingrid.

"And then what?" Mia said.

Stacy gave her a quick glance. Ingrid was starting to recognize that Stacy and Mia didn't have much in common, mostly just the fact that they were both her friends. "Then what?" Stacy said. "Get a job, of course."

"With an eighth-grade education?" Mia said. "What kind of a life is that?"

Stacy's faced reddened. "Good enough for lots of people," she said.

Mia shrank back into her puffy pink jacket. She was tiny, with fine bones and features. Stacy was big and strong, hardest kicker by far on last fall's U-13 girls' soccer team – a team that had gone all the way to the regional final, losing 2–1, their lone goal coming from Ingrid late in the game, first ball she'd ever headed in.

They dangled in silence – not one of those comfortable silences – Ingrid dragging the toes of her boots in arcing patterns in the snow. After a while Stacy said, "My dad dropped out at sixteen."

"Yeah?" Ingrid said.

"Yeah," Stacy said.

"Oh," said Mia.

Mr. Rubino was an electrician, and a great one in Ingrid's opinion. People still talked about how he'd lit the Cheshire Cat's smile in the Prescott Players' production of *Alice in Wonderland*, somehow leaving a big yellow grin in empty black space. Plus he'd built a kick-ass entertainment center in the basement of the Rubinos' house, a nice house in the Lower Falls neighborhood, not far from Joey's. Maybe they weren't rich, but comfortable, right? And kids liked going over to the Rubinos', a pretty happy place, despite some problems with Stacy's older brother Sean, recently sent away to a military academy in Tennessee or Oklahoma or somewhere.

"That's that," Ingrid said. "I'm dropping out in two and a half years."

Stacy laughed, then Mia. The mood got back to normal.

Or maybe not quite, because Mia said, almost to herself, "My dad's got an MBA from Harvard Business School." The unspoken part – *for all the good that did us* – was very clear. Mia's dad lived in New York, and almost a year after the divorce he and Mia's mom were still fighting – sometimes in e-mails that got copied to Mia, maybe by mistake.

"We'll all drop out," Stacy said. "Start a restaurant in Hawaii."

"Surfin' Fish Burgers," Mia said.

More laughter: Stacy had a great laugh, real loud. The bell rang. They hopped off the swings, started back to the building. Stacy remembered something and ran ahead.

"Did your mom say anything about Joey?" Ingrid said.

"Joey?" said Mia. "Why would my mom say anything about Joey?"

"He was with me on Sunday," Ingrid said. "At the falls."

"Huh?" said Mia.

"We went snowshoeing in the woods," Ingrid said. "All the way to the falls. Your mom was there. She didn't mention it?"

"My mom was at the falls?"

"In the picnic area," Ingrid said. "She said you were at the library."

"I was," Mia said. "But she was going to Stop & Shop after she dropped me off."

"Maybe she had extra time," said Ingrid.

"Are you sure it was her?"

"We talked. She met Joey."

Mia had beautiful eyes, huge and pale blue. Now they seemed to cloud over.

"Get a move on, you two," said Ms. Groome, math teacher, waiting at the door, knitting needles sticking out of her coat pocket. Winter light glared off fingerprint smears on her glasses. "Or would you prefer a nice long detention?"

*   *   *

"Afternoon, petunia," said Mr. Sidney, the school bus driver, as Ingrid got on board. Girls were always "petunia" to Mr. Sidney, guys "guy", as in "any more shenanigans and you're walkin', guy".

"Hi, Mr. Sidney," said Ingrid, moving toward the back. Stacy was already there, saving a seat for her, but – what was this? A grown-up in one of the front seats? And what was more, a grown-up she knew – Mr. Samuels, editor, publisher, arts and entertainment critic, and chief reporter for the Echo Falls *Echo*. Oh my God. Was he doing some follow-up on Brucie? "Up Close and Personal with Echo Falls's New Young Funnyman" or something even more nauseating? She glanced ahead, saw Brucie a few rows behind Stacy, patting his head while rubbing his stomach for maybe the zillionth time. But Mr. Samuels didn't seem aware of him. He was writing in a notebook, the words tiny and precise, his long nose close to the page.

"Ah," he said, looking up. "Hello, Ingrid."

"Hi, Mr. Samuels," Ingrid said.

"How's that grandfather of yours?"

"Pretty good."

He laid the notebook on his knee. "Actually, you might be able to do me a favor in that regard. Got a moment?"

Ingrid exchanged a puzzled look with Stacy, sat beside Mr. Samuels. He was a tiny old guy with alert little eyes and a scrawny neck, knew more about the history of Echo Falls than anyone, a fact that had helped her more than once in the recent past.

"Right now," said Mr. Samuels, lowering his voice as the door closed and Mr. Sidney shifted into gear, "you're wondering what the heck this old coot is doing on the school bus."

"Everything but the old coot part," said Ingrid.

Mr. Samuels laughed. "A career in journalism – don't rule it out," he said. He angled the notebook so she could see. At the top of the page he'd written *WW2*. "Planning a special multipart series," he said, "celebrating all the World War Two veterans from Echo Falls. The ones still alive and kicking, that is."

Was it Ingrid's imagination, or did Mr. Sidney floor the pedal, just for a split second, at the words *alive and kicking*? His Battle of the Coral Sea cap was perched low on his head. Mr. Sidney and Grampy had been at a place called Corregidor together, something Grampy never talked about.

"What they did then and where are they now – profiles," said Mr. Samuels. "Today I'm working on Boom Boom Sidney."

"Boom Boom?" said Ingrid. "I thought his name was Myron."

"Yup," said Mr. Samuels. "But he had a great slapshot when he was a kid."

Ingrid glanced at Mr. Sidney. His shoulders were so bony. "How many are there?" she said.

"How many vets left?" said Mr. Samuels. He slapped his bony knee. "There's a reporter's question for you. Answer: five, four still living in Echo Falls or close by. Three from the Pacific theater, two European, and so far I've got promises of cooperation from all but one."

He didn't have to name the non-cooperator.

"I've sent letters," said Mr. Samuels. "No response. And the phone just rings and rings out there."

"No voice mail," Ingrid said.

"Be a shame to leave him out of the piece," said Mr. Samuels. "Probably the only surviving genuine World War Two hero in this part of the state."

Grampy a war hero? First she'd heard of it. "What did he do?" Ingrid said.

"Exactly what I'm trying to nail down," said Mr. Samuels.

"Then how do you know he was a war hero?"

"Lots of good journalism schools, but if I were you, I'd take a shot at Columbia, Ingrid," said Mr. Samuels. He rose, tightened the knot of his skinny brown tie, already pretty tight. The bus slowed down. "As for how I know, that's a matter of public record. Aylmer Hill of Echo Falls, Connecticut, was awarded the Medal of Honor in August of 1945."

"For what?" Ingrid said.

"The details are sketchy," said Mr. Samuels, moving past her. "That's why I'd like to talk to him." He handed Ingrid a white envelope. "Maybe you could see that he gets this, even somehow persuade him to actually read it." The bus stopped. "Thank you, Boomer," he said, getting off.

"Anytime, Red," said Mr. Sidney.

Mr. Samuels had no hair at all. Did these old-timers feel awkward with their childhood names clinging to them? Ingrid had felt awkward with hers from the get-go, partly because of how it sounded, partly because it came from Ingrid Bergman, the impossibly beautiful actress in *Casablanca*, Mom's favorite movie. Maybe Ingrid was the kind of name that got better with age. Nothing she could do about it anyway: her all-out seventh-grade effort to make people call her Griddie had been shot down by everyone, even complete strangers.

"What was that all about?" said Stacy when Ingrid went back and sat beside her.

"Not sure," Ingrid said. "What's the Medal of Honor?"

"That video game," said Stacy. "Sean used to play it all the time."

"I'm a level-ten master," Brucie called out from the back.

"Zip it, guy," said Mr. Sidney.

five

the gingerbread house stood deep in the woods. House, woods, and sky: all dark. Ingrid had no intention of going any closer, was not about to take even one more step. But there was nothing she could do about it. With a sickening shudder, the forest floor was suddenly on the move, like a conveyor belt, taking her faster and faster to the gingerbread house. A pair of yellow eyes appeared behind an upstairs window.

"Ingrid! Wake up!"

She opened her eyes. Her room was dark and shadowy. The bedside clock read 6:05, almost an hour before she had to get up for school. Dad stood in the doorway.

"Where are those minutes?" he said.

"Minutes?" Her voice was croaky. She cleared her throat, tried to clear her mind of forest-dream remnants. "What—"

"That Grampy was supposed to sign," Dad said, his tone sharpening. "Don't tell me you forgot them."

Ingrid rubbed her eyes, all crusty. "I guess I must have, but—"

"Damn it," Dad said. "Get up, then. You're coming with me."

"Where?" Ingrid said.

"The farm," Dad said. "You can run in and get them. I'll drop you off at school."

"But—"

"You heard me."

"Hey," called Ty from his room across the hall. "Trying to get some sleep here, if that's okay with you guys."

They rode in silence. Dark clouds sagged low in the sky, and something between rain and snow was falling in thick streaks. Sleet? Freezing rain? Was there a difference? Ingrid glanced at Dad, decided not to ask. He was far away. The windshield wipers went back and forth, back and forth, reminding her of this old movie she'd seen, featuring a metronome and someone locked in a closet. It got darker. All the cars had their headlights on. Staying in bed till noon sounded just about right.

Dad pulled into Grampy's long driveway, parked in front of the house. "Be quick," he said.

No smoke rose from the chimney. "What if he's not up?" Ingrid said.

"He's up," said Dad. At that moment his cell phone rang. "Hello," he said. And then, "You've got the wrong number." He clicked off.

Ingrid got out of the car, knocked on Grampy's door. After a moment or two it opened, and there was Grampy, dressed in canvas pants and a flannel shirt with the sleeves rolled up. His feet were bare; Ingrid noticed how finely shaped they were, and how they didn't seem old at all.

"Hey, kid," he said. "This is a surprise." He looked past her, saw the car, rolled down his left sleeve, but not before Ingrid saw a Band-Aid on the inside of his elbow, partly covering a yellow bruise.

"I forgot those minutes, Grampy," she said.

He looked vague. "Minutes?"

"That you were supposed to sign."

"Paperwork," Grampy said. "Had it up to here." He went back into the house, soon returned with the envelope. Ingrid was sliding it into her pocket when she felt something else in there. What was this? Oh, yeah: Mr. Samuels's letter.

She handed it to Grampy. "This is from Mr. Samuels," she said.

Grampy gazed at it with narrowed eyes. "What does that nosey parker want?"

"To interview you," Ingrid said.

"Never could mind his own business," said Grampy.

"But he runs a newspaper, Grampy. So isn't it his business to—"

"Newspaper? You call that rag a newspaper?"

Ingrid kind of liked *The Echo*, strangely boring and interesting at the same time, but she didn't argue. "I promised him that you'd at least read the letter," she said. "He's doing a special edition about World War Two veterans from Echo Falls. Five of you are left, and all the others said yes."

Grampy went still.

"Mr. Samuels says you were a hero," Ingrid said.

Grampy's gaze, very distant, slowly returned to the here and now. He looked down at her. "Isn't this a school day?"

"Yeah."

"Then scat." Grampy closed the door, taking Mr. Samuels's letter with him.

Ingrid went back to the TT. Dad, on his cell phone, snapped it shut as she opened the door.

"Got 'em?" he said.

She nodded. He started the car, and soon they were back on 392, that same streaky stuff falling from the sky, Dad driving Dad style, two fingers on the wheel and fast.

"What did Grampy do in the war?" she said.

"The war?" said Dad. "He doesn't talk about it."

"What's the Medal of Honor?"

"For courage in battle," Dad said.

They crossed the bridge. Down below, the streaky stuff hit the water and disappeared, not even making any splashes.

"Mr. Samuels says Grampy won it," Ingrid said.

"I've heard that too," Dad said.

"And?"

Dad glanced at her. "I told you – he doesn't talk about it."

Silence after that, almost all the way to Ferrand Middle. Sometimes, when Dad was annoyed or tense or maybe for other reasons Ingrid didn't know, a lump of muscle appeared in the side of his face, right above the hinge part of the jaw. Ingrid saw it now.

"Dad?"

"Yeah?" He slowed down behind the line of buses; one of the Dratch twins had his face pressed to the back window, his features – distorted to begin with – distorted even more.

"I saw a nice picture of your mom at Grampy's."

Dad stared straight ahead, didn't say anything.

"You look a bit like her."

Dad nodded, very slightly.

"How old were you when she...?"

Dad turned to her, the lump of muscle even more prominent. "You know all this, Ingrid."

True. There were all these facts of family history she'd grown up with, but maybe she didn't understand their – what was the word? It came to her, a word recently heard from the lips of Mr. Porterhouse: "Boston Tea Party, significance of." *Significance,* that was it. For the first time, Ingrid realized *significance* contained *sign* and understood what the word really meant.

"Eight?" she said.

"Six," Dad said, his voice going high-pitched all of a sudden. They crept forward behind the buses. Dad said, "Six" again, this time in his normal voice.

"It was cancer?" Ingrid said.

"You know all this," said Dad again. The line moved another foot or two. "Jump out here. I haven't got all day."

Ingrid slung on her backpack and walked into the school. Someone said something to her, but she didn't take it in: she was thinking about what it would be like for a six-year-old boy growing up alone with Grampy out on the farm. Somewhere behind her, tires squealed on icy pavement.

"What the heck," said Mr. Santos, straying from the script right from the top, "are we gonna do? How're we sposta feed the kids when there's no grub for ourselves?" He held up his hands, palms up, sustaining the gesture for what seemed to Ingrid – seated on a stool next to Brucie in the corner of the stage where Hansel and Gretel's bed would be – a very long moment.

"In the morning, Husband," said Meredith O'Malley in her breathiest little whisper, "let's take them into the woods and leave them while we go off to our work. They will not find their way home, and our problem will be solved." She smiled a big bright smile; months of cosmetic dental work were finished at last, and her teeth were huge and sparkling.

Jill Monteiro, watching from a plush red seat in the fifth row of the Prescott Hall theater, said, "If we could hold it right there for a sec?"

The woodcutter's little family gazed out at her – all except Brucie, who was peering into his shirt pocket.

"Meredith?" said Jill.

"I'm sorry," said Meredith. "Was it too … too outside in?"

"No," said Jill. "Not that."

"Oh, good," said Meredith. "I've been trying to work more outside in lately, without overdoing it, of course." She paused. No one spoke. Brucie had discovered something sticky in his pocket, was pulling it out. "Like Sir Laurence Olivier?" Meredith said. "I read his bio."

"Wasn't it great?" said Jill. "I love how much thought he put into his characters."

"Isss it safe?" said Brucie, shoving the sticky mass back in his pocket.

Jill glanced at him in surprise. "And on the subject of character, Meredith, what can you tell me about the woodcutter's wife?"

Meredith put her index finger – the nail long and bright red – to her chin. "She's very hungry," she said.

Jill clapped her hands, eyes shining. "Excellent," she said. "You're very hungry, all of you – keep that in mind. It's no accident that the witch's cottage is edible."

Wow, Ingrid thought. Jill was amazing. An idea hit her. "Maybe we should all lose some weight before opening night," she said.

"Huh?" said Mr. Santos.

"Nice idea, Ingrid," Jill said, "but in this case I think costume and makeup will do the trick."

"Whew," said Meredith under her breath.

Jill rose, came forward, enthusiasm radiating off her. "We've got hunger, Meredith," she said. "What else?"

Meredith did that index-finger-to-chin thing again, but this time it didn't work. After a while, Ingrid said, "Is she the mother or the stepmother?"

"Great question," Jill said. "In early versions of the story she's the mother. Only later did she turn into the stepmother. Any idea why?"

"Typo?" said Brucie.

"How was rehearsal?" Mom said.

"Good," said Ingrid.

Mom drove her MPV van Mom style, hands in proper ten-minutes-to-two position, speed limit never exceeded. Only a few minutes after five, but the sky was already black, except for some purple edging in the west; Ingrid confirmed the direction on her compass ring.

"I never liked that story," Mom said.

"'Hansel and Gretel'?"

Mom nodded. "I could never believe any parents would abandon their children like that."

"That came up," Ingrid said. "Jill was trying to get Meredith to sound meaner. She said not to forget how hungry they all were."

"Still," said Mom.

They drove in silence for a few minutes, a light snow starting to fall, the flakes strangely black in the headlights. The expression on Mom's face changed in a way Ingrid had seen before. She knew what was coming next: as a kid Mom had been great at memorizing poems, had all this poetry inside her.

Mom spoke. She had this special poetry voice, quiet but musical, almost sounding like a different person.

> *"And I saw in the turning so clearly a child's*
> *Forgotten mornings when he walked with*
>   *his mother*
>   *Through the parables*
>   *Of sun light*
> *And the legends of the green chapels…"*

The legends of the green chapels: was that meant to be something about the woods? Ingrid didn't think she'd ever heard anything so beautiful in her life; so different from those woods in "Hansel and Gretel."

"Hunger or not," Mom said, turning in to the driveway at 99 Maple Lane, "I just don't buy it."

"nigel could use a walk," Mom said on Saturday morning.

Ingrid, eating waffles – a brilliant invention, in her opinion, with those square depressions, kind of like rice paddies, so perfect for containing mini lakes of buttery maple syrup – glanced over at Nigel. He lay in his usual spot by the water bowl in the sunny corner of the kitchen nearest the stove, one eye fully closed, the other open maybe the tiniest crack, front paws stretched out comfortably. Was walking on his mind?

"What about Ty?" Ingrid said.

"He's got Five Tools," Mom said, stuffing real estate listing sheets into her bag. "I'm dropping him on the way to work." Five Tools was a baseball skills class run in the winter at the rec center by Mr. Porterhouse, who was also the varsity coach at Echo Falls High. The five tools were hit, field, throw, and two others Ingrid couldn't remember at the moment, all of which Ty, or Ty and Dad, or maybe just Dad, were determined to improve before spring tryouts.

"He doesn't want a walk," Ingrid said.

"Ingrid." Mom glared at her; that hardly ever happened, or never. Then her eyes got liquid. "I don't have time to argue." She grabbed her bag and left the room. What the hell?

"Okay, okay," Ingrid said. "On your feet, Nigel."

That one eye, maybe open a crack? Now it was squeezed shut, beyond any possible doubt, closed so tight it must have hurt.

"Where to?" said Ingrid.

Nigel, on his leash, stood at the end of the driveway at 99 Maple Lane, damp nose in the air, one forepaw raised alertly in that misleading way he had, as though he were a pointer or some other clever dog. In fact, he came from no particular breed, in some way didn't remind Ingrid of dogs at all, was more like Nigel Bruce, the tweedy, bumbling actor in old black-and-white movies who had played Dr. Watson to Basil Rathbone's Sherlock Holmes; Ingrid had the complete collection. Nigel had strayed into their lives in the fall, almost immediately chewing up Mister Happy, the teddy bear Ingrid had slept with almost all her life.

"Come on," she said. "Which way?"

But Nigel just stood there, frozen in position like some street performer. Left meant a long uphill walk that would take them to a park where Nigel liked to dig deep holes; right led past Mia's house at the corner of Maple Lane and Avondale. Maybe Mia was home, could be persuaded to come along. Ingrid gave Nigel a little tug to the left. He immediately veered right. Reverse psychology: she knew Nigel.

He ambled in his unhurried way, not bothering to sniff the air or chew snow chips or do any other doggy things. Oops – not so fast. Outside 113 he suddenly lifted his leg, like it had been jerked up by a puppeteer, and peed on the FOR SALE sign – RIVERBEND PROPERTIES, CALL CAROL LEVIN-HILL. Mom hadn't shown 113 in weeks despite two price cuts, and Ingrid had overheard her telling Dad she was worried about losing the listing. "Not here," Ingrid said, dragging Nigel away. He left a spotted yellow trail in the snow.

They came to Mia's. It was a nice house, a lot like Ingrid's – same builder, Mom said – but smaller and darker, under some overhanging trees. A big black car stood out front. Like Sherlock Holmes – if there'd been cars in his day, which she was pretty sure there weren't, since everyone was always coming and going in hansom cabs or dogcarts – Ingrid noticed the license plate: New York. A man sat behind the wheel staring straight ahead. At that moment Nigel suddenly picked up speed, almost reaching his top gear, a kind of waddling sprint, and turned up the path to Mia's front door, pulling Ingrid along. She remembered he'd been here a few weeks ago. Had Mia given him a treat? Oh, yeah, half a hot dog – Hebrew National, his favorite brand. So who was doing the reverse psychology?

Nigel started up the front steps, wheezing with excitement. The door opened, and Ingrid heard Mrs. McGreevy, very loud: "… and not one minute later."

Mia came out; in the background stood Mrs. McGreevy,

arms folded across her chest. They both looked startled to see Ingrid; both went pale at the same time.

"Hi," said Ingrid. What was going on? No clue. She plowed on. "Want to come for a walk with Nigel?"

"I, uh," said Mia. She pointed with her chin at the black car. "My dad's taking me to lunch."

Ingrid turned. "That's your dad?" He was still staring straight ahead. Mrs. McGreevy was in the doorway now, an angry blush rising up her neck.

"Yeah," Mia said. "He's got a meeting in Hartford."

"Um," said Ingrid. A few moments passed, all awkward. "Call me later."

"Yeah," said Mia. She got in the front seat of the car. It drove away. Mia looked very small.

Ingrid felt a tug on the leash: Nigel, still in search of that Hebrew National. Ingrid tugged back. "C'mon, boy." The door closed in his face, very close to a slam.

"Divorce," Ingrid explained to Nigel, halfway through a very long walk, easily their longest ever, a walk that took them out of Riverbend, onto Main Street, and all the way to the village green. But divorce meant nothing to Nigel, or to any other dog, even the smartest that ever lived. Did it have meaning for any animals at all? Ingrid scrolled through a few in her mind – bears, deer, crocodiles, geese. She just didn't know enough about their habits to know. And even with those creatures that mated for life, none of which came to mind at the moment, did the offspring bother to stick around for more than a few weeks or months? Life was pretty short for most animals; on the other hand, they had no inkling. Only human beings had inklings about the end part. What was that quote? Ingrid remembered Mom saying it, one day when she'd dragged the whole family to some strange art thing at the Wadsworth Museum in Hartford: *Death casts a shadow backward.* Oh, boy. "Death casts a shadow backward," she said to Nigel. His stubby tail drooped, but that might have been because he was getting tired. Ingrid was feeling a little droopy herself. She started to wheel Nigel around and head for home, and then noticed two men standing in front of the Civil War monument on the green.

Two old men. One she recognized: Mr. Samuels. He had a camera in his hand and was motioning for the other man to move closer to the monument, a column with names carved into the stone and a bronze soldier above – turned green by time – his cap and shoulders topped with snow. The other old man, also completely bald but otherwise nothing like Mr. Samuels – much taller and wearing a black patch over one eye – backed up a step and said something in an annoyed way. Ingrid caught the words, "… got all day."

Something about the scene grabbed Nigel's interest. His tail rose back to full height (not very high) and started wagging a bit. He tugged Ingrid toward the monument.

"Nigel!" she said, in a loud whisper meant only for his floppy ears. But both men heard and turned to her.

"Why, Ingrid," said Mr. Samuels, lowering the camera. "Is that you?"

"Hi, Mr. Samuels."

"What luck," he said. "Here's someone I'd like you to meet."

Ingrid went over, Nigel trotting along, all at once obedient, even eager to please. For a moment it looked like he was about to greet Mr. Samuels or the other man, but instead Nigel went right by them and lifted his leg at the base of the monument.

"Ingrid," said Mr. Samuels, "this is Mr. Cyrus Ferrand."

Ferrand? The Ferrands were the richest family in town. Ingrid had been friends with Chloe Ferrand when they were little, and Dad worked for her father at the Ferrand Group, but Ingrid had never heard of Cyrus Ferrand. He glanced down at her for the briefest moment, glanced with that one eye, dark at the center, with lots of red veins crisscrossing the white part.

"Major," he said.

"Yes, of course," said Mr. Samuels. "Major Ferrand. That's the whole point of the exercise."

Exercise? Ingrid wasn't following.

"In fact, what an opportunity," said Mr. Samuels, putting a hand on Ingrid's shoulder and gently nudging her closer to Major Ferrand. "A picture of the two of you together might be just the ticket."

"Ticket to what?" said Major Ferrand, edging away.

Mr. Samuels crouched in front of them, snapped a picture. "Very nice," he said. Then Nigel, circling back from the base of the monument, looped the leash around Major Ferrand's legs. Major Ferrand kicked free, gave Nigel a one-eyed glare, a glare that turned to something else, inquisitive and probing.

"The point is, Ingrid," said Mr. Samuels, "Major Ferrand is one of the Echo Falls Five."

"The Echo Falls Five?" said Ingrid.

"The surviving World War Two veterans," said Mr. Samuels. "Major Ferrand spends most of his time on Anguilla now, in the Caribbean, but he's Echo Falls born and bred, still has a cottage on the Ferrand estate. What makes Ingrid's appearance here so serendipitous, Cyrus, is the fact that she's the—"

Major Ferrand interrupted. "This dog has no tag," he said.

"It's on his other collar," Ingrid said. The one with the broken clasp, no good with the leash; but how was it his business?

Nigel gazed up at Major Ferrand. Suddenly he cringed – Ingrid had never seen him cringe before – then made a little whiny noise and sidled over behind Ingrid.

Major Ferrand licked his lips; his tongue was pointy, the color of chalk. "My housekeeper's dog—" he began.

"Enough dog talk, if you don't mind," said Mr. Samuels. "What I'm trying to tell you, Cyrus, is that Ingrid is Aylmer Hill's granddaughter."

Major Ferrand's one eye closed, and stayed closed for a long moment. Then it opened and gave her a careful look. "What a small town," he said.

"Exactly," said Mr. Samuels. "That's the meaning of the whole piece, the strength of old bonds. A piece for which I'm very much in Ingrid's debt, I might add."

"How is that?" said Major Ferrand.

"Because Aylmer has agreed to be interviewed on his wartime exploits."

"He has?" said Ingrid.

Mr. Samuels nodded happily. "Wouldn't have happened without your help."

Major Ferrand looked a little pale. His mouth opened, closed, opened again. "His wartime exploits?" he said.

"Practically a scoop," said Mr. Samuels. "In all these years he's never given a single interview – there's just no information at all. And he promised a bombshell – his very word. Now how about you two move the ittiest bit closer together and I'll shoot a couple quickies? Page-one smiles, now – top of the fold."

Ingrid posed with Major Ferrand, their arms touching. His trembled: she could feel it through her jacket. Living most of the time in the Caribbean now, he'd probably forgotten what winter was like.

seven

"it's so dark," Ingrid said. "How will we ever get out of these woods?" Maybe too whiny and helpless? No one liked a wuss, and Gretel wasn't necessarily a wuss, just a little kid. Sitting at the kitchen table, alone after school on Thursday, Ingrid popped the top on a Fresca and tried again, making herself sound more composed. "It's so dark. How will we ever get out of these woods?"

The door to the garage opened and Mom came in, a bag with *Ta Tung* on the side, written to look like Chinese letters. "What was that, Ingrid?"

"It's so dark. How will we ever get out of these woods? Or: It's so dark. How will we ever get out of these woods?"

Mom put the Chinese food on the table, kicked off her shoes, slipped into her sheepskin slippers, as she always did the moment she got in the door. Her eyes grew big and dark: Ingrid could tell she was replaying the *Hansel and Gretel* dialogue in her mind.

"The second one's supposed to be more composed," Ingrid said.

Mom nodded. "But it sounds like you're asking directions."

Ingrid laughed. "So something in between?"

"Try that."

Ingrid tried something between helpless fear and asking for directions. Maybe it worked. There was just the slightest tremble in her voice; she sounded scared but brave at the same time, or at least trying to control her fear. Did real bravery start like that, just making a bit of an effort to control fear?

"Much better," Mom said.

"Is that working inside out or outside in?" Ingrid said.

Mom didn't answer. She just smiled, came closer, and kissed Ingrid on the forehead.

"What?" said Ingrid. Even Mom, of all people, was sometimes hard to understand.

"Where's the Mongolian ribs?" Ty said, peering into the cardboard containers.

"They didn't have them tonight," Mom said. "I got the crispy duck instead."

"What do you mean, they didn't have them?" Or something like that – hard to tell with Ty's mouth stuffed full of egg roll, those delicious Ta Tung egg rolls, blackened at the ends.

"Eat what you're given," said Dad.

After that there were just chewing sounds, Ty's dominating. Was he having another growth spurt? He seemed bigger than he was just last week, or even yesterday.

"Try the crispy duck," Mom said, passing it around the table. "It's really good."

Dad helped himself and said, "Any results, kids?"

Results meant grades on quizzes, tests, exams, or papers.

"Nope," said Ty.

"Nope," said Ingrid. Not strictly true, if you were counting today's seventy-one on Ms. Groome's math test, but a test wasn't really a *result*, not if result meant "final result," and weren't final results what counted? Bottom line, walk the walk, just win, baby – wasn't that the American way? Therefore bringing up this little matter of the seventy-one, one of those neither-here-nor-there grades that could only lead to lots of bothersome speculation, was almost un-American. Algebra, week after week, month after month, this dogged quest for X, bound to be fruitless, like all those other quests: Loch Ness monster, Holy Grail, origin of the— Whoa. Dad was eyeing her in a way that suggested some follow-up question might be next. Ingrid blurted the first thing that came to mind: "Who's Major Ferrand?"

"Tim's great-uncle," Dad said; Tim was Dad's boss at the Ferrand Group. "Where'd you hear about him?"

"I met him." Ingrid explained about walking Nigel, the Civil War monument, Mr. Samuels.

"Funny," Dad said. "I don't think he's been here in years."

"Maybe it's because of the series," Ingrid said.

"What series?" Dad said.

"On World War Two veterans, in *The Echo*. Mr.

Samuels is interviewing him. And Grampy."

"Grampy agreed to an interview?" Dad said.

"That's exciting," Mom said. "I can't wait to read it."

"Did he kill anybody?" Ty said.

"What kind of a question is that?" Dad said.

Ty shrugged. "A war question."

"Don't be a smart-ass," said Dad. He checked his watch, took a deep breath. "Have to go in to the office for a while."

"Now?" said Mom.

"Won't be long," Dad said. He put on his jacket, went into the garage. "*Echo*'s still in the driveway," he called. "One of you come get it." Then came the throaty rumble of the TT's engine; it faded away. Mom had her head cocked to one side, as though listening.

"Rock, paper, scissors," said Ty.

He'd won the past three – paper every time, which was so unlike him, Ty being a rock or scissors type.

"On three," said Ingrid.

"One, two—"

Ingrid: scissors. Ty: rock. Rock? Now he went back to rock? How did he know to do that? She walked outside to get *The Echo*. Hey! Maybe she was in it – that picture of her with Major Ferrand. Or was it too soon? She was bending down for the paper, wrapped in orange plastic, when a car went by, going pretty fast. Ingrid glanced up. A green hatchback: the streetlight shone for a moment on the face of the driver, Mrs. McGreevy. She was hunched forward, holding the wheel tight in both hands.

Ingrid took *The Echo* inside, slipped off the wrapper. She wasn't above or below the fold, at least not on the front page. Instead there was a picture of a prematurely gray man. Ingrid recognized him. The headline – a big one for *The Echo* – read: CONSERVATION AGENT MISSING. Underneath it:

> *Harris H. Thatcher, assistant agent for the Department of Conservation in Echo Falls, has been missing for two days. According to his wife, Marleen Thatcher, Mr. Thatcher was last seen leaving for work on his bicycle on Tuesday morning. Mr. Thatcher, an energetic proponent of alternative transportation, is a common sight for Echo Falls residents, riding his bike in all weather.*
>
> *"This just isn't like Harry," said Mrs. Thatcher. "I'm worried sick." Gilbert L. Strade, chief of the Echo Falls police, said that a missing persons report has been filed and an active investigation is under way. He urged anyone with information to call the station. When asked if the police were currently pursuing any leads, the chief had no comment.*

"Hey, Mom, did you see this?"

But Mom was on the phone. "I'm afraid that's under agreement," she was saying, "but we have another nice listing in that area." She made an impatient not-now gesture to Ingrid. With surprising quickness

Nigel snatched the last egg roll off the table and ran from the room.

"Gum?" said Joey.

"Thanks," said Ingrid, taking a stick. Lunch line, cafeteria, Ferrand Middle: The special of the day was labeled TUNA CASSEROLE. Ingrid and Joey were near the back of the line, but no one had ordered it yet.

"Guess what," Joey said.

"What?"

"There's an old Indian trail."

"Yeah?"

"It's on this old map."

"What old map?"

"On the Internet. There's this old map of Echo Falls on the Internet. See what I'm saying?"

"No."

"My dad showed me. He—"

"Wait a minute – is the farm on it?"

"Farm?"

"My grandfather's."

"Oh, yeah, sure. The Indian trail cuts right across his fields."

"It does?"

"We could try it out," Joey said.

"Next," said the lunch lady.

Joey pointed to the tuna casserole.

"You're having that?" Ingrid said.

Even the lunch lady looked surprised. Joey didn't seem to notice. "Tomorrow, maybe," he said. "Like, on our snowshoes."

"Goes without saying," said Ingrid.

"How about I drop you right here?" said Chief Gilbert L. Strade, slowing down and pulling over. He was a big man with a big jaw, strong nose, and prominent brow ridge, but his voice was soft, at least in Ingrid's experience. They were on 392, not far from Uncle Lou's Hot Dog Emporium at the town line, now boarded up for the winter.

Ingrid, following Chief Strade's direction, sat up front. Joey, sitting in back, hunched over his map printout, said, "Are we near Old Post Road?"

The chief tapped the windshield. Joey looked up. A road sign a few yards ahead read OLD POST RD. "Oh," he said.

A crackle came from the cruiser's radio, and a voice said, "Bike path check complete, Chief. Negative."

The chief spoke into his transmitter. "Okay, Sarge," he said. "See you at the station." He clicked off, turned to Ingrid. "Missing persons case."

"Harris H. Thatcher?" said Ingrid. "I saw it in *The Echo*."

"Left home on his bike," said the chief. "Had special tires for snow – packed snow, at least – rode in all weather."

"So you think he had an accident?" Ingrid said.

"Nothing else to go on," said the chief. "Sometimes middle-aged guys just disappear, start a new life somewhere, but Thatcher doesn't seem like the type."

"What's the type?" Ingrid said.

A little smile crossed the chief's rough face, very

68

brief. "Disappointed guys," he said. "Guys in a jam. Guys tired of responsibility. No sign Harry Thatcher fits any of that, plus he was all wrapped up in community issues."

"Can we get going?" Joey said.

The chief glanced at Joey in the rearview mirror, looked like he was about to say something, did not. Ingrid and Joey climbed out of the cruiser, strapped on their snowshoes. The chief's window slid down.

"See you back here in two hours," he said.

"Okay," said Joey.

"Wearing your watch?" the chief said.

"Course."

"Let's see."

Joey pulled up the sleeve of his jacket. His wrist was bare; he looked surprised. But Ingrid was wearing hers – a red watch with the word *Rollexx* on the face, Christmas present from Stacy and one of her favorite possessions, especially since Stacy had forgotten to re-move the $9.95 price sticker from the back. She wore it every day; Sherlock Holmes, who had a pocket watch, always said he needed data, and if time wasn't data, what was?

The chief wheeled around and drove back toward town. Joey stuffed the map in his pocket and climbed up onto the snowbank that ran beside Old Post Road, gazed across a snowy field. "We should see a— There it is."

"What?"

"That old gate."

A falling-down wooden gate stood in the middle of

the field, looking kind of strange all by itself, unattached to a fence or anything. They walked through it, found the path well packed by skiers and snowmobilers, easy going.

"How do we know this is an Indian trail?" Ingrid said, taking off her mitten to check the compass ring.

"Says on the map," said Joey. That expression she heard from time to time, *begging the question*? Ingrid understood it at last.

They went up a long slope, not steep, then back down, across a wide valley and up a round hill. At the top Ingrid looked down and saw a fence, then another rise, and in the distance a crooked storage shed, an orchard, a rusty-red barn, an old farmhouse. A view she'd never seen from this angle; it took her mind a few moments to spin it around. "Grampy's farm."

"Yup," said Joey, like he was Kit Carson or some other famous guide. Ingrid punched him on the arm, an affectionate sort of punch. "Ow," said Joey. Their breath clouds rose and came together in the air.

They went down to the fence, saw that the trail swerved and ran parallel to it, avoiding Grampy's land. Joey took out his map. "The real trail cuts right through to the river," he said.

"Let's take it," said Ingrid. "Grampy won't mind."

Joey raised one of the strands of wire. They climbed through, started up the rise, now in unpacked snow, not easy. Joey pulled ahead, reached the storage shed ahead of her.

"Hey," he called.

"What?"

"Your grandfather left his bike out."

"He doesn't have a bike."

But when Ingrid got to the shed, she saw a green bike leaning against the side, its big fat tires sunk an inch or so into the snow.

"Maybe we should put it inside," Joey said.

But the door was padlocked shut.

"I wonder—" Ingrid began.

Joey, looking past her, interrupted. "What's that?"

Ingrid turned. Not far away lay a round depression, the size of a small pond. All covered with snow now, but Ingrid realized this must be the sinkhole where last fall she'd helped Grampy rearrange the surface level a little bit, as he'd put it – a rearrangement that had involved four sticks of dynamite. At the near edge of the depression she could make out something red and black. A long twisted form, actually, that made her think, *Scarecrow, knocked down by the wind.*

But she'd never seen a scarecrow on the farm. That was thought two. And then came a third. Red and black: Grampy often wore that red-and-black-checked lumber jacket. The next thing Ingrid knew she was running, running in her snowshoes, which should have been awkward and clumsy, but she didn't even seem to be touching the ground. And almost every step brought a new horrible detail: a man; white hair; blue skin; very still.

"Grampy! Grampy!"

Dead, yes. A man, yes. A white-haired man, yes. But not Grampy. And also not a stranger: Ingrid had seen this man before, once in person and once on the front page of *The Echo*. It was Harris H. Thatcher, missing conservation agent.

She felt Joey's hand on her shoulder. Her first dead body, but Ingrid knew Harry Thatcher was dead, beyond a doubt. It wasn't just the blueness of his frozen skin, or the emptiness in his staring eyes. Something else – some huge thing she couldn't name – was gone. For a moment there wasn't a sound. It was then that Ingrid noticed red drops in the snow, three of them, the size of quarters.

"Oh my God," said Joey.

"Don't go any closer," Ingrid said. She checked the time on her red Rollexx.

eight

ingrid knocked on Grampy's door.

"Grampy? Grampy?"

No answer. The house was silent.

"Maybe he's asleep," said Joey.

"He doesn't sleep in the day," Ingrid said. But then she remembered how she'd gone upstairs and found him sleeping in his plain little bedroom. She knocked harder. "Grampy! Grampy!"

No answer.

"Maybe he's not home," Joey said.

Of course. She hurried over to the barn, Joey following. They looked through a window. The tractor and the old Caddy stood in their usual spots, but the pickup wasn't there. The piglet saw them and came to the front of his pen.

"Have you got a key to the house?" Joey said.

"No."

"So, um, what do we…" His voice wasn't quite steady, but that might have been from the cold.

Ingrid looked at her watch. "We go back to Old Post Road," she said, "and wait for your dad." Her voice wasn't quite steady either. The thermometer on the side of the barn read nineteen degrees. Yes, the cold; that was it.

Chief Strade knelt beside the body of Harris Thatcher, Ingrid and Joey behind him.

"Touch anything?" he said.

"No," said Joey.

"When did you find him?"

Ingrid told him, to the minute.

The chief took off his glove and touched Harris Thatcher's neck. His finger looked so red and alive next to Harris Thatcher's blue skin.

"He's dead, right, Dad?" said Joey.

The chief nodded.

"That's what we thought," Joey said. "Ingrid and me."

The chief looked over his shoulder at Joey, a hard expression on his face, the first time Ingrid had seen it. Joey's eyes shifted away. The chief turned back to the body, examining those three red spots in the snow. He took out his radio, started giving orders. After only a few seconds Ingrid heard a distant siren. The chief spoke into his radio.

"No damn siren."

It went silent at once.

They all went back to staring at the body. Ingrid couldn't help herself: you could study a dead person way more intently than a living one, or at least she could, without fear of rudeness. Was rudeness even possible with only one of you there? So Ingrid stared, and she noticed things: like the waffle soles on Harris Thatcher's boots; the top of a spiral notebook sticking out of the back pocket of his jeans; and how his left arm was twisted underneath him in a way that would get uncomfortable after just a few seconds.

"I don't think it's a bike accident," Joey said. A long pause, and then he added, "'Cause of how the bike's over by the shed. Which is, like, pretty far from here."

No one spoke for a moment or two. Then the chief said, "No, not a bike accident."

That was when Ingrid saw something in Harris Thatcher's white hair, just behind his ear, something that might have been a mud spatter. "What's that in his hair?" she said.

"Not in his hair," said the chief. "Under it." A squad car appeared on 392, blue light flashing but siren off. "That's an entry wound, Ingrid."

"You mean…?"

"He was shot," said the chief.

The wind stirred, not much, but enough to ruffle Harris Thatcher's white hair, cover up the wound. That movement, the ruffling hair, somehow made Ingrid feel that all this staring was rude no matter what, and she looked away.

"When did it happen?" she said.

The chief's heavy eyebrows rose. "That's for the medical examiner to say," he said. "But I'd guess three or four days ago."

"Then—" Ingrid began, but stopped herself.

"Go on," said the chief.

"I was just wondering when it last snowed," Ingrid said.

"So was I," said the chief.

"What are you guys talking about?" said Joey. "Who cares when it snowed?"

"Well, Ingrid?" said the chief.

"If it hasn't snowed since ... since this happened, then there might be lots of clues around."

"Like?" said Chief Strade.

"Like footprints, for one thing," said Ingrid. "But all I see are the two snowshoe tracks, Mr. Thatcher's steps coming from the shed, and yours, Mr. Strade."

The chief nodded. "And the snow doesn't look fresh to me," he said.

"So?" said Joey.

"So he wasn't shot from close range," Ingrid said.

"Maybe he shot himself," Joey said.

The chief's eyes, small eyes but bright, swung for a moment toward Joey, seemed to soften slightly. "Can't rule that out, son," he said. "Not yet."

"But?" said Ingrid.

"But it's an unusual placement for a suicide wound," the chief said. "Not impossible, just unusual."

"And if it's suicide," said Ingrid, "where's the gun?"

"Maybe underneath him," Joey said.

Ingrid looked down. One gloved hand, the right, was visible; the body covered the left hand. She saw that the spiral notebook in the back pocket was open at an inside page. Bending a little she could actually read what was written on the top line: *sinkhole – dynamite???*

"Maybe," the chief said. "We'll soon find out." More flashing blue lights appeared on 392.

A snowplow came, cleared a path all the way from the end of Grampy's driveway to the shed. Then came a squad car with Sergeant Pina – who umped Little League games and played Santa in the Christmas parade – and some other cops. And after that another squad car, an ambulance, and the medical examiner. They got busy with yellow tape, measurements, cameras.

"You kids wait in Sergeant Pina's car," said the chief.

Ingrid and Joey got in the back of the cruiser. Sergeant Pina left the engine running, heat on – a good thing, since they were both shivering. Joey took an energy bar from his pocket, broke it in two, offered half to Ingrid.

"Not hungry," she said.

Joey ate both halves. Outside, Chief Strade pulled the spiral notebook out of Harris Thatcher's pocket, riffled through a few pages, and slipped it into a clear plastic bag. Sergeant Pina and the medical examiner – a big woman in a puffy ski jacket – turned Harris Thatcher's body over: no gun underneath. The angle of his head, his legs, his arms, including the twisted-up one – everything stayed in the exact same position.

"He's frozen," Ingrid said.

Joey put his hand on hers, kept it there. After a while they stopped shivering. The chief and the medical examiner knelt over the body. The medical examiner, wearing surgical gloves, parted Harris Thatcher's blue lips. The chief said something. The medical examiner was about to reply, but at that moment everyone stopped what they were doing and turned their heads up the hill, toward the orchard.

Ingrid followed their gaze, saw the pickup coming down the freshly plowed track, Grampy at the wheel, going fast. He stopped by the shed – very abruptly, the pickup slewing to one side – got out, and walked down to Chief Strade. Grampy wasn't wearing a hat, gloves, or a jacket, just a white T-shirt; a white T-shirt with black dress pants and black dress shoes, which was kind of strange.

Ingrid opened the door in time to hear him say, "What's going on here? Why are all you people on my land?"

"Mr. Hill?" said the chief. "I'm Gilbert Strade, chief of police."

Grampy looked him in the eye. "I know who you are," he said. "You didn't answer my question."

Ingrid got out of the car.

"The answer is we found a dead man on your property," the chief said.

"Impossible," said Grampy.

"I'm afraid not," said the chief. "As you can see." He raised the yellow tape. Grampy walked under. The medical examiner rose, leaving the body by itself in the snow. Grampy glanced down at it.

"Do you know this man?" said the chief.

Grampy took a second look, and his eyes narrowed. "Oh, yes," he said. "I know the son of a bitch."

Then there was silence out in Grampy's fields, although the wind rose a little higher, stirring the soft white hair of both of them, Grampy and the dead man.

Ingrid moved closer.

Soft white hair, and Chief Strade's voice was soft too. "You had some problems with him?"

"Nothing I couldn't handle," said Grampy. His bare arms were covered in goose bumps from the cold, but those cords of muscle, so amazing in an old man, still stood out.

"Handle in what way?" said the chief.

"That's between me and him."

Ingrid took one or two more steps, found she'd somehow gotten under the yellow tape and was now standing next to Grampy. He didn't notice her.

"Is there anything you want to tell me?" said the chief.

"About what?" said Grampy.

Chief Strade motioned toward the body. "About him," he said.

"What would I want to tell you about him?" said Grampy.

"Anything that might help with the investigation," said the chief.

Grampy got that had-it-up-to-here look on his face. "Can't help you," he said.

"There's a dead man on your property," the chief said. His voice stayed quiet but changed in a way that was hard to define, growing harder, hinting – at least to Ingrid – of something dangerous, even violent, inside. For the first time ever, she felt a little afraid of Chief Strade. Grampy was just being Grampy, but only Ingrid knew that. How did he appear to all these people – the chief, the medical examiner, Sergeant Pina, and the other cops? She could feel them watching him.

"I can see that," Grampy said. "What's he doing here in the first place?"

"I was hoping that was one of the questions you could help me with," said the chief. He gazed directly into Grampy's eyes.

Grampy gazed right back. "I already told you I can't," he said.

"The kids say you weren't home earlier today," the chief said. "Mind telling me where—"

"Kids?" said Grampy. "What kids?"

"Grampy," Ingrid said, practically right beside him.

He glanced down, blinked. "Ingrid? What are you doing here?"

"We were snowshoeing on the old Indian trail," Ingrid said. "Me and Joey." Joey, standing by the open door of the cruiser, one foot still inside, made a little half wave that looked kind of ridiculous at a moment like this. "We found the body and went to tell you, but you weren't home."

"Old Indian trail," said Grampy. "What nonsense."

Ingrid had no idea what Grampy meant by that; all she wanted was for him to calm down a bit, but she couldn't think of anything to say, not with everyone watching. She touched Grampy's arm. Still goose-bumpy, but it felt surprisingly warm, even hot. He had another one of those Band-Aids on the inside of his elbow, a bigger one this time, with a blue bruise, meaning it was new.

"Mind telling me where you were, Mr. Hill?" said the chief.

"None of your business," Grampy said.

"Grampy," Ingrid said in a low voice, meant only for him.

He showed no sign of having heard her, but Chief Strade said, "You might want to get back in the car, Ingrid. Sergeant Pina will take you kids home."

Get in the car? And leave Grampy alone? How could she do that?

"I..." Ingrid began. *I what?* For a moment it was too much – all those uniforms, those three red holes in the snow, the body – and Ingrid almost caved, even felt her lower lip tremble. But hardly at all; no one could have seen.

"She's my granddaughter," Grampy said. "If there's any driving to be done, I'll be doing it."

"No problem," the chief said. "Then if you don't mind waiting up at the house, Ingrid?" He turned to Joey. "Get in the car, Joe. And close the door." Joey got into the car and closed the door.

"Drive him home, Chief?" said Sergeant Pina.

The chief nodded. Sergeant Pina drove the cruiser up the plowed track toward Grampy's driveway. Ingrid could see Joey watching her through the rear window.

She turned and started up toward the house. The last thing she heard was the chief asking Grampy if he owned any firearms, and Grampy's reply: "What I own I own by right."

nine

ingrid stood in the kitchen, waiting for Grampy. The sinkhole, depression, whatever it was, couldn't be seen from anywhere in the farmhouse, the view blocked by the orchard and maybe too distant in any case. A black suit jacket hung over a chair by the table, also a navy-blue tie with dull gold stripes. Ingrid had never seen Grampy in a jacket and tie before. This particular tie looked nice. She went over, felt it: silk, very soft. And beside the chair stood a closed suitcase, like Grampy had just come back from a trip. Probably not an airplane trip – no baggage tag wrapped around the handle.

Kind of surprising: she didn't remember Grampy ever going on trips. On the other hand, maybe he did. No reason she'd know – sometimes she might not see him for a week or two, or even more. So he'd come back from some trip – but not a long one, because who would take care of Piggy, last animal on the farm – come back probably tired and a little disoriented, the way you felt

82

after a trip, only to find that whole crime-scene thing going on. Anyone might have been crabby.

So stop worrying this minute, Griddie.

She stopped worrying, or almost. Just before the complete stoppage of worry, she opened the broom closet. The broom closet was where Grampy kept his guns. The .22 rifle, which he'd taught Ingrid how to shoot – Grampy was a crack shot – stood in its place in the corner; the .357 automatic lay on the shelf. Ingrid took out the rifle, finger off the trigger, muzzle pointing straight down, and opened the bolt. The gun was unloaded. She put it back and closed the door, leaving the .357 untouched. Grampy had said she wasn't ready for the .357. Besides, Harris Thatcher had been shot from a distance – the absence of tracks proved that, as long as there'd been no fresh snow. Distance shooting wasn't what the .357 was for. On the other hand – uh-oh – she'd seen Grampy fire it once, last fall when a dangerous woman named Julia LeCaine had invaded his home. Worry, not quite gone, started making a comeback.

Ingrid returned to the table, touched the tie again. Maybe the biggest surprise, that Grampy would own such a fine tie. She was raising the end to check the label when the door opened and he came in.

Grampy stopped dead. "What are you doing here?"

Ingrid let go of the tie. "Just looking at your tie, Grampy. It's nice."

He closed the door with his heel, came to the table. "Tie?" he said. Then he noticed it. Grampy grabbed the tie, balled it up, stuffed it in the pocket of his black dress pants. "That doesn't explain anything," he said.

"What do you mean?"

"About what you're doing here."

"Waiting for you to drive me home, Grampy."

There was a pause. Grampy let out his breath, long and slow like a sigh, except there was no sound. "Right," he said. "How old are you again?"

Ingrid laughed. That was a joke he sometimes played, forgetting her age. "Thirteen," she said.

Grampy nodded, still poker-faced. "Too young to drive in this Godforsaken state," he said. "Let's get going."

"What do you mean, 'Godforsaken state'?" Ingrid said.

"Look around," Grampy said.

They went out, got in the pickup. Had he really forgotten her age this time? "Are you okay, Grampy?"

"Why wouldn't I be?" said Grampy.

He drove down the driveway, onto the road, toward town. Snow started falling, a few flakes at first, then more. "What did the chief say, Grampy?"

"Nothing important," said Grampy. "Damn nuisance."

He didn't speak the rest of the way. When they were almost home, Ingrid tried, "I hear you're going to do an interview with Mr. Samuels." Grampy just grunted.

Ingrid tossed and turned.

"Never seen woods like these," said Grampy.

Neither had Ingrid: trees hundreds of feet tall, packed closely together, darkness everywhere, as though an enormous black umbrella hung overhead. But every-thing would be all right. Grampy had the .22 in one hand and the .357 in the other.

"We'll be all right," Ingrid said. "You've got the guns."

"Ammo's no good," said Grampy. "Warranty's up a long time ago."

"We've got no ammo?" Ingrid said.

Grampy said, "I'm scared."

"But what about the Medal of Honor, Grampy?"

No answer. The trees closed in.

Ingrid awoke in a sweat. She reached for Mister Happy; gone, of course, gnawed to nothing by Nigel.

"Nigel?"

She switched on the bedside light. No Nigel.

"Nigel?"

Then from out in the hall came a slurping sound. She got up, went into the bathroom, found Nigel drinking from the toilet.

"Nigel!"

He raised his head, snout dripping, glanced over at her, and went back to what he was doing, stubby tail wagging. Ingrid turned on the tap, poured a glass of water, drank it down. She saw herself in the mirror: dark shadows under her eyes, damp twists of hair stuck to her forehead. She looked like an actress made up to play a haunted version of her.

Nigel stopped drinking, sidled over, leaned against her leg. Maybe it made no sense, but she felt a little better.

Ingrid started back toward her bedroom. In the hall she heard voices from Mom and Dad's bedroom.

Mom said, "What do you think happened?"

Dad said, "Hell if I know."

Mom said, "What should we do?"

Dad said, "I don't have all the answers."

Mom said, "I know, Mark. I just—"

Dad said, "I'm tired. I need my sleep."

After that, silence. Ingrid went back to bed. There was a dream she could sometimes make happen: Griddie on a snug and unsinkable boat in a wild ocean storm. She tried it now, picturing herself in a cozy bunk belowdecks. It worked. She fell into a deep sleep, the wind rising around her.

Mom and Ty were already gone when Ingrid came downstairs Monday morning. Mom had to go right by Echo Falls High on the way to the Riverbend office, so Ty got a ride every day. Ingrid took the bus.

Dad was usually at the kitchen table, in one of his beautiful suits, drinking coffee and reading *The Wall Street Journal*, but not today. She heard TV voices, followed them into the living room. Mom didn't like having a TV in the living room, so they'd compromised with a very small TV on rollers kept behind a big plant unless someone – meaning Dad – was watching.

He was watching now, on his feet, just a few feet from the screen. And on the screen? An overhead shot, maybe taken from a helicopter, of a barn, orchard, snowy fields, yellow tape: Grampy's farm. "… awaiting the results of ballistics tests," an announcer was saying. "According to Echo Falls police chief Herman Strade, there are no suspects at this time. Back to you, Rita."

Dad switched it off, turned, and saw Ingrid.

"His name's not Herman," she said.

"They get everything wrong," he said. "The more you—"

The doorbell rang.

"Who could that be?" Dad said. He checked his watch.

"Want me to answer it?" said Ingrid.

"I'll get it," Dad said.

She followed him into the front hall. Dad opened the door. Chief Strade stood outside. He took off his chief's hat with the gold braid. "Good morning, Mark," he said.

Dad nodded.

The chief's eyes shifted for a moment to Ingrid, then back to Dad. "As I'm sure you know, I'm investigating the Thatcher murder. The body was found on your father's farm."

"I'm aware of that," Dad said.

The chief put his hat back on. "I'd like your permission to talk to Ingrid."

"About what?" Dad said.

Permission? Ingrid didn't understand: She often talked to Chief Strade. He was Joey's dad, for God's sake, plus they'd kind of helped each other on a couple of recent crimes.

"About certain events that may pertain to the case," the chief said. He looked at Ingrid again. "Since she's a minor, I'd like your permission." His voice was formal, like they were strangers.

They all just stood there. Across the street the Grunellos' door opened, and Mrs. Grunello, in a fluffy turquoise robe, came out carrying a recycling box. Her gaze went to the scene in front of 99.

"All right," Dad said. "But I have to be present."

"Of course."

"And I also have to leave for work in fifteen minutes."

"That's fine," the chief said. "I had no intention of making Ingrid late for school."

They sat at the kitchen table, Dad in Dad's chair, Ingrid in Ingrid's, Chief Strade in Mom's. Now the chief had his hat in his lap.

"That must have been upsetting," he said. "When you found the body."

"Of course it's upsetting," said Dad. "She's a thirteen-year-old kid."

The chief eyed Dad, a cool, appraising look. Ingrid didn't want him looking at her father like that. She said, "Yes, it was upsetting. Joey was upset too."

"I'm sure," said the chief. "Which one of you was the first to recognize the body?"

"Realize he was dead, you mean?"

The chief shook his head. "Realize who it was," he said.

"I guess me," said Ingrid.

"And how did you know?" the chief said.

How had she known? Because she'd seen Harris Thatcher before – once the man himself, once his photograph in *The Echo*. "He was in *The Echo*," she said. "On the front page."

The chief smiled. "You read *The Echo*, Ingrid?"

"Yes."

"And you recognized his face from the photo in *The Echo*?"

"Yes," said Ingrid. "The article about how he was missing."

"In my experience," the chief said, "most of the photos in *The Echo* could be a lot clearer."

Ingrid didn't say anything. Dad glanced at his watch.

"I understand *The Echo*'s running a series on the World War Two veterans, including your grandfather," the chief said.

"Yes," Ingrid said.

"Any idea what he did in the war?"

"Not really," Ingrid said.

"Aren't we getting a little far afield?" said Dad.

"Maybe," said the chief. "We're still waiting to hear from ballistics."

"Lost you there," said Dad.

"Just that it's early in the investigation," said the chief. "There are a lot of possibilities. What I'm trying to get straight now is how Ingrid identified the body."

"And she just told you," Dad said. "From *The Echo*." He rose. "Is there anything else?"

The chief stayed where he was, seated in Mom's chair. His face wore an expression she'd never seen on it before, almost sad. "So that's the story, Ingrid?" he said. "You recognized Harris Thatcher from *The Echo*?"

One little nod and this would be over. Ingrid nodded.

Now the chief did look sad, no doubt about it. He reached into an inside pocket and withdrew a spiral notebook. An everyday object, nothing to be afraid of, but Ingrid was suddenly afraid.

"This notebook was recovered from the body," the chief said. He leafed through. "It appears to be a work diary, where Mr. Thatcher kept track of developments in his caseload. This is from an entry a couple weeks back." The chief licked his lips and started reading. He turned out to be not a very good reader at all, monotonic and even stumbling over a word or two. "'Mr. Hill refused to have any discussion whatsoever. He produced a rifle of some kind, and the situation might even have turned violent if a girl that I took to be his granddaughter hadn't intervened.'"

The chief looked up. "Was that you, Ingrid?"

Now came a second nod, and with it the knowledge that this was far from over.

"So is it possible," said the chief, "that your identification of the body was based in fact on your presence during this incident at the farm?"

One more nod – against her wishes, involuntary, but it happened anyway: an admission that she'd been caught in a lie by the chief of police.

The chief closed the notebook. "Any idea what kind of rifle your grandfather produced?" he said.

"This discussion is over," said Dad.

The chief looked at him, his eyes so cold, his face so hard, that he almost seemed like someone else. "One last thing," he said. "The ME puts the time of death somewhere between noon and three p.m. on Tuesday. Care to tell me where you were then?"

"Me?" said Dad. "Is that a serious question?"

"Very," said the chief.

Dad gave the chief a hard stare. But then he seemed to have a thought, and his eyes shifted. "I was with a client," he said.

"Name and location?" said the chief.

Now Dad wasn't coming close to meeting the chief's gaze. He looked embarrassed, even … even guilty. "I'll fax that to you from the office," he said.

The chief went away. Dad closed the door, rubbed his face, and turned to Ingrid.

"Keeping any other secrets?" he said.

Ingrid shook her head. But was Dad keeping secrets? Was there any way he could have had anything to do with this? No. The murderer was a good shot and Dad had no interest in guns, had never even fired one in Ingrid's experience. Plus he had no connection at all to Mr. Thatcher, and if anything was probably on Mr. Thatcher's side when it came to Grampy's behavior. But then why had he looked so guilty?

"If you are, tell me now," Dad said. "I don't want Grampy hiding behind you."

How could Dad say such a horrible thing? Didn't he know his own father? Ingrid felt herself going red-hot. "Grampy doesn't hide behind anybody," she said. "And he would never—"

Dad's cell phone rang. He took it from his pocket,

checked the number, didn't answer. Ingrid seized the moment to run up to her room, slamming the door behind her.

ten

"what's wrong?" Stacy said.

Recess. They dangled on the swings, Ingrid and Stacy. A bunch of boys were shooting hoops on the paved court nearby, Joey one of them. He didn't look her way.

"Nothing," Ingrid said.

"That conservation guy?" said Stacy.

"What makes you say that?"

"There are all these rumors."

"Like what?"

"I don't know," Stacy said. "About him getting shot on your grandfather's farm."

"That's not a rumor."

"Don't get mad at me." Stacy cracked her gum.

"I'm not mad at you. What rumors? Who's spreading them?"

"I wouldn't say exactly spreading them. But Sergeant Pina and my dad are buddies. They go hunting in Maine, stuff like that."

"And?"

"And he came over last night. With his truck. My dad was putting new speakers in it. Sergeant Pina, I'm talking about."

"And?"

"And when they were going into the garage, I heard Sergeant Pina say that Mr. Thatcher was a jerk."

"Yeah?"

"Yeah. Way too much of a – what's the word? – when it comes to the environment."

"What's the word?"

"Begins with a *z*."

The only *z* word Ingrid could think of was *zero*.

"Rubs people the wrong way for no reason. That was what my dad said. Sergeant Pina said he wouldn't really blame your grandfather if … you know. Then they started with the drills and I didn't hear any more."

"He didn't do it," Ingrid said.

Stacy glanced at her sideways, said nothing.

"No way," Ingrid said. "The bullet hole was toward the back of the head and the shooter wasn't close-up. That's how a coward kills. Not Grampy."

Stacy put her hand on Ingrid's shoulder, gave it a squeeze – a hard squeeze, Stacy not knowing her own strength. "I believe you," she said. "One hundred percent."

"*Zealot,*" said Ingrid.

"Huh?"

"That's the *z* word."

The bell rang. They lined up. Ingrid found herself near Joey. Their eyes met.

"Hi," said Ingrid.

"Um," said Joey. He looked away.

"Two lines," said Ms. Groome. "And you there – dispose of that gum."

"What gum?" said Stacy, swallowing it.

Ingrid had rehearsal after school. A real bad rehearsal: she forgot everything – her marks, her cues, her lines. Jill wrapped it up early. Ingrid went into the lobby of Prescott Hall, prepared for a long wait. But Brucie's father, coming in the door, said, "Hello, Ingrid. Your mom called and asked if I'd drop you off."

"Oh," said Ingrid. Did Mom even know Rabbi Berman? She herself had met him only once, in the Prescott Hall parking lot.

They got in Rabbi Berman's car, Ingrid, at Rabbi Berman's insistence, in front, and Brucie in back.

"How was rehearsal?" said Rabbi Berman.

"Good," said Ingrid. She remembered that he was a rabbi and added, "Thanks." She didn't know anything about rabbis, had no idea what to expect. She glanced at Rabbi Berman. He looked like all the other dads.

"Music?" he said, sliding a CD into the player.

"Sure," said Ingrid.

"No," said Brucie, a groaning kind of no.

Music started playing.

"Love Bob Dylan," said Rabbi Berman.

Brucie didn't say another word the whole way. Ingrid had never heard him so quiet.

Ingrid got out of the Bermans' car in front of 99 Maple Lane. Ty was standing in the driveway. Not coming or going, just standing there, almost as though he was waiting for her. She walked up to him. Were those tears in his eyes? That made no sense: Ty wasn't a crier.

"Ingrid?" he said.

"Yeah?"

"Grampy's in jail."

"In jail?"

"Locked up," Ty said. "For murder."

"Oh, no," Ingrid said. Then she, also not a crier, was crying too. Ty put his arms around her. They hugged. "He didn't do it," Ingrid said.

"But he's got no alibi," said Ty.

Ingrid backed up. "How do you know?"

"There's a lawyer inside," Ty said. "I heard them talking."

"Mrs. Dirksen?" said Ingrid. Mom had told Ingrid that Mrs. Dirksen was their lawyer for wills and stuff.

Ty shook his head. "This guy came from Hartford." Ingrid noticed what she should have seen right away, a huge SUV in the driveway. The vanity plate read: LEAGLE. For no reason she could express it gave her a bad premonition.

Ingrid and Ty went in the house. Mom and Dad were in the dining room with a man in a dark suit, papers spread all over the table. Dad had that lump of muscle showing over his jaw. Mom had the two vertical lines deep in her forehead. Only the lawyer seemed relaxed. Ingrid wasn't good at guessing the ages of adults, but right away she wished the lawyer looked older. He wore a nice suit – as nice as the ones Dad wore, but more tight fitting. His hair was somehow scruffy and well cut at the same time, like a lawyer in a movie.

"Kids," said Dad, "go upstairs. We'll talk later."

Going upstairs? Unbearable. "But Grampy's in jail," Ingrid said. "What are we going to do?"

"We're taking care of it right now," Dad said. "Go upstairs."

Taking care of it how? Very wrong for her to blurt that question out at a time like this, and Ingrid fought to keep it in.

The lawyer turned to her. "Is this Ingrid?" he said.

"Yes," said Ingrid.

"I'll need to speak to her."

Getting talked about in the third person: Ingrid didn't like that. "What about?" she said.

"We can get to that a little later," said the lawyer.

Mom said, "Mr. Tulkinghorn is going to get Grampy out on bail. Please do as your father says."

Ty turned to go. Ingrid followed. But at the door she stopped – just couldn't help herself – and said, "Is it true Grampy has no alibi?"

"Ingrid!" Dad said. "You're wasting precious time."

She left the room, feeling horrible.

Upstairs, an IM from Stacy (Powerup77):

Powerup77: hey

Gridster22: hey

Powerup77: whassup?

Gridster22: not much

Powerup77: you ok?

Gridster22: no alibi

Powerup77: i heard

Gridster22: ???

Powerup77: it was on tv

Gridster22: omg

Powerup77: cant account for where he was

"Ingrid?" Her door opened and Mom came in. "Mr. Tulkinghorn wants to talk to you now."

"About what?" Ingrid said.

Gridster22: cu

"I'm not sure," Mom said.

"What should I say?"

"Just answer his questions honestly," Mom said.

"But—"

"He's on our side," Mom said. "He's our lawyer."

"Mom?"

"Yes?"

"Is he any good?"

"Of course he's good, Ingrid. Dad checked."

How did you check something like that? Ingrid didn't know. "Chief Strade really believes Grampy shot Mr. Thatcher?" she said.

"I don't know what he believes," Mom said.

"But it's impossible," Ingrid said.

Mom took her hand. Mom's hand was icy cold. She gazed deep into Ingrid's eyes, as though searching for something. "Is it, Ingrid? Apparently Grampy kept guns at the farm. I never knew that."

True. And also Mom didn't know that Grampy had taught her to shoot the .22, lining up Coke bottles on the fence behind the barn, and how she was actually a pretty good shot; and maybe even worse, from Mom's point of view, how all that shattering glass was kind of thrilling. Ingrid had a strange vision of how life might be. You came in incapable of speech. Then you started talking. Pretty soon you said something that was wrong, or that someone thought was wrong, and then you were in your first snarl. The more you talked, the more chances you'd end up in more snarls, snarls spiraling within snarls. And by the time you were old, say Grampy's age – how snarly could things get by then?

Ingrid said nothing. She went downstairs with her mother.

"Hi, again," said Mr. Tulkinghorn. Just the two of them in the dining room: He'd wanted to talk to her alone. "I'm Rex Tulkinghorn." A little pause. Was she supposed to say something yet? "And you're Ingrid," he went on. "I've already heard a lot about you."

Like?

But Mr. Tulkinghorn didn't go there. He opened a briefcase – all the papers had been cleared away, the table now bare – and took out a yellow notepad. "I'm a lawyer," he said. "You're aware of what lawyers do?"

They ask patronizing questions? Ingrid kept that thought to herself and just nodded.

"Your parents have hired me to defend your grandfather. Any help you can give me will be much appreciated."

"He didn't do it," Ingrid said.

"Oh? You know that for a fact?"

Ingrid explained: first, how the footprint evidence proved that Mr. Thatcher had been shot from a distance; second, that Grampy would never do something so cowardly – and practically from behind, as well.

"You're quite the little detective," said Mr. Tulkinghorn. "What can you tell me about your grandfather's guns?"

Ingrid glanced into the hall, saw no one, but thought she could feel Mom close by. She kept her voice down. "He has a .22 rifle and a .357 handgun."

"Licensed?"

"I think so." *What I own I own by right.*

Mr. Tulkinghorn made a note on the yellow pad. He was one of those people who pressed way too hard with the pen, almost piercing the page. "And what about a .30-06 Springfield rifle, possibly equipped with a sniper's scope?"

"No," Ingrid said.

"No he doesn't have such a weapon, or no you never saw one?"

"I never saw one."

Mr. Tulkinghorn made another note in his heavy-handed way.

"Why?" Ingrid said. The word just popped out, unbidden.

He glanced up, annoyed. "Why what?"

"Why are you asking about this other kind of rifle?"

"Because the ballistics tests came back," said Mr. Tulkinghorn. "The bullet was a .30-06."

Not a .22 or a .357! "That's good, right?" Ingrid said.

Mr. Tulkinghorn reached into his briefcase, removed a printout. Reading upside down, Ingrid made out the heading: *United States Army.* "Aylmer Hill was issued a Springfield M1903A4 .30-06 sniper rifle with an M73B1 2.5 power sight on February 1, 1942," said Mr. Tulkinghorn, following his finger across the page. He looked up, his eyes cold. "There's no record of that rifle ever being returned to the Army quartermaster prior to Aylmer Hill's discharge on September 3, 1945." He took out a picture, showed it to Ingrid: an old-fashioned-looking rifle with a brown wooden stock and a skinny black scope mounted on the top. "Ever heard the word *implication*?" he said.

Ingrid nodded.

"Know what it means?"

She nodded again, not patiently.

"Then you see the implication of this combination of facts," said Mr. Tulkinghorn.

"That he took the rifle home with him from the war and used it to shoot Mr. Thatcher?" Ingrid said.

"Exactly," said Mr. Tulkinghorn. "So I'll ask once more: have you ever seen, or has your grandfather ever referred to, a gun like this?"

"No," said Ingrid, her voice suddenly sounding very loud in the dining room. This guy was supposed to be on their side. That thought was followed by another: *What will the other side be like?*

"If there is such a weapon," said Mr. Tulkinghorn, "the police will find it. They're out there now, turning the place upside down."

"Can't you stop them?" Ingrid said.

"They've got legal warrants, signed by a judge," said Mr. Tulkinghorn. "Think they're going to find anything?"

"Never."

"Never because such a weapon doesn't exist, or never because it will be so well hidden?"

"The first one," said Ingrid, barely aware that her chin was tilting up in a defiant sort of way.

Mr. Tulkinghorn put everything back in his briefcase. "If we go to trial," he said, "it's your parents' wish that I do all I can to keep you off the stand."

"But why?" said Ingrid. "I want to help."

"It's not the defense that would be calling you," said Mr. Tulkinghorn. "Unless I can work some kind of deal, you'll be a witness for the prosecution."

"I don't understand."

"They'll want the court to hear all about the argument between your grandfather and the victim." He rose, adjusted his tie. "And there's no law that says a grandchild can't be called to testify against a grandparent."

The argument: Ingrid remembered, practically word for word, including Grampy's reply when Mr. Thatcher said he'd be back, with a warrant if necessary. *I wouldn't do that if I were you.* She tried to imagine how that would sound, coming from her on the stand. Oh, God.

Ingrid rose too. "What are we going to do, Mr. Tulkinghorn?"

"Get him out of jail, first," said Mr. Tulkinghorn. "Then go at him one more time about an alibi."

"An alibi – meaning he was somewhere else at the time, couldn't have done it?"

Mr. Tulkinghorn nodded. "The medical examiner has established the time of death – something I could possibly attack at trial, but it would be pointless without more cooperation from your grandfather."

"What do you mean?"

"Death occurred between the hours of noon and three p.m. on Tuesday. I asked your grandfather where he was at that time."

"And?"

"And he said, 'None of your business.'" Mr. Tulkinghorn started from the room. "Only he put it more strongly than that."

Mom and Dad were in the hall. "Here's your retainer," Dad said, handing Mr. Tulkinghorn a check. Mr. Tulkinghorn looked at it carefully and slipped it into his pocket.

eleven

from *The Echo* – exclusive:

Aylmer Hill of Echo Falls, charged in the murder of conservation agent Harris H. "Harry" Thatcher, was released on $500,000 bail last night. Asked for comment outside the Echo Falls police station, Mr. Hill shook his head and got into a car driven by his lawyer, Rex Tulkinghorn of Heep and Tulkinghorn in Hartford. Mr. Tulkinghorn was quoted as saying, "My client will be vindicated."

According to sources close to the Echo Falls police, Mr. Thatcher, acting several weeks earlier on an anonymous tip concerning unauthorized use of explosives on Mr. Hill's farm off Route 392, made an attempt to interview Mr. Hill. A furious conversation ensued, and Mr. Thatcher was threatened with armed violence. Sources say Mr. Hill has offered no explanation as to his whereabouts at the time of the murder, established by the medical examiner as last Tuesday, February 11, between noon and 3:00 P.M. The murder weapon has not yet been found. Mr. Hill was a noted marksman in World War II.

Ingrid read the article twice. "How come there's nothing about the Medal of Honor?" she said. No one answered. She was alone in the house except for Nigel, relaxing by his bowl. "How come, Nigel?" she said. "It would help if people knew he was a hero." Nigel found the energy to raise his tail an inch or two off the floor. Gravity took over from there, and it flopped down with a soft thump.

Ingrid read the article once more, forcing herself to go really slow this time. She found a pencil and paper, made some notes.

1. anonymous tip?
2. where was Grampy?
3. murder weapon?

Now she had a list, but what did it mean? Her mind refused to make those three questions add up to anything. What did Sherlock Holmes do in baffling situations? Sometimes he took cocaine; that was out. Or he played his violin; Ingrid, although she liked belting out songs in the shower, had no musical ability whatsoever. But sometimes Holmes went for a walk, maybe taking

Dr. Watson along.

"Nigel? Let's go."

Nigel started to roll over, like he was getting up on command, big surprise. But he stopped halfway, remaining on his back, paws comfortably folded in.

"Nigel!"

She ended up dragging him outside on his leash, stubbornly supine all the way to the end of the driveway. After that he got up and trotted along beside her in his waddling way. "Let's start with the anonymous tip," Ingrid said.

Memory was tricky. There seemed to be two kinds. First: the kind that popped up all on its own, usually very clear – like Joey's face, just before he'd moved in for that snowshoe kiss that hadn't happened. Second: the kind you had to go rooting around in your brain for, which usually ended up being pretty blurry – like facts about the Whiskey Rebellion. The anonymous tip problem involved both kinds of memories.

The dynamiting down at the sinkhole – that was the first kind of memory, sharp and unbidden. At the time, last fall, Grampy had been worried that the Ferrands and maybe other rich developers were trying to get hold of his land for building condos. He'd come up with this plan to make the sinkhole deeper, turning it into a permanent pond. That was the dynamiting part. Four sticks! After that – a huge boom and then a rising mud cloud that came splattering back down – Ingrid had waded in and planted eastern spadefoot toad eggs. The endangered eastern spadefoot toad: that was the whole point. In the spring, when they hatched and endangered toads started hopping around, any development plans would be … how had Grampy put it? Something about fish? Dead as a mackerel – that was it.

But the anonymous tip part: that was the other kind of memory, the kind you had to hunt for. Ingrid didn't know who the tipster was; she just had a vague sense of some tiny fact buried way down deep in her… All of a sudden she pictured a phone. Not just any phone, but that old-fashioned black one with the rotary dial in Grampy's kitchen. And she fished up the memory, maybe not word for word, but close enough.

Ring.

"Aylmer?"

"This is his granddaughter."

"Bob Borum here, over on Robinson Road. You people hear a boom? Thought it was a transformer, but we've got electricity."

"So do we."

"Not to worry then."

"'Bye, Mr. Borum."

"Bob Borum," Ingrid said. Nigel paid no attention. In fact, he was chewing on a— "Nigel!" And what was this? They were practically at the end of Avondale, almost at the strange cul-de-sac part where three new houses had been standing for months on bare, unland-scaped lots, waiting for buyers. Ingrid pulled Nigel around. A car was coming toward them, not fast, a beige car, small and boxy. As it went by, it slowed even more, and the driver looked out, a fat-faced guy with greasy blond hair and a cigarette in his mouth.

"Come on, Nigel." Ingrid headed for home, picking

up the pace. She heard the car rounding the cul-de-sac, returning. Then she felt it moving up alongside her, now at a walking pace. She looked sideways. The window rolled down. Then a weird thing happened. The driver leaned out, his face partly obscured by a camera. His finger pressed the button, once, twice, three times. Ingrid actually flinched, and Nigel, not much of a barker, barked real loud. The car sped up, zoomed away. Fast, but not so fast that Ingrid, with her sharp eyes, wasn't going to read that license plate. Except she couldn't: it was smeared with mud. The car turned the corner and disappeared, leaving a cigarette end spinning in the air.

The cigarette was lying on the road, still smoking slightly, when Ingrid got there. She bent over it, read the label: Virginia Off-Label Generics. Ingrid didn't want to touch it, not even with her mittens on.

She and Nigel walked back home. "What a creep!" she said. Nigel barked. "Good boy." One little thing: from the way the camera was pointing, kind of down, Ingrid got the idea that either the creepy guy was a bad photographer or he'd been deliberately taking pictures of Nigel.

No one home. A note from Ty on the fridge: *Greg's.* The phone was ringing. She picked it up.

"It's me," Joey said. "Joey."

"I know."

"You sound a bit, um. Like you're mad or something."

"Yeah," said Ingrid. "I'm mad."

"At me?"

"Yeah, at you."

"Oh," he said, almost inaudible.

"Not just you," Ingrid said. "Everybody."

"Huh?"

"Figure it out."

"Well," said Joey, "me because I haven't been – you know…"

"Talking to me?"

"That's it. The thing is…"

Silence. It went on and on.

"The thing is what?" Ingrid said.

Joey got even quieter. "My dad…"

More silence.

"Your dad told you not to talk to me?" Ingrid said.

"Yeah. But not like to be rude or anything. 'Don't be a jerk about it.' That's what he said."

"Why?" Ingrid said.

"I guess because he didn't want me to be not polite," Joey said. "He has this thing about not—"

"Not that," Ingrid said.

"Why not to talk to you, you mean?"

"What else?"

"Oh," he said. "The main point, right?"

"Right." Hard to stay angry at Joey, but she still felt lots of anger inside her, burning away – a feeling she wasn't that accustomed to, and didn't like.

"Because of the case," Joey said.

"The case," said Ingrid, "is about my grandfather."

"A man died, too," said Joey. "Mr. Thatcher."

"I know," Ingrid said. The truth was she hadn't had one single thought about Mr. Thatcher, or his wife, quoted in *The Echo* as being so worried when he was still missing, or any family or friends he might have had. But Grampy didn't do it. "Why didn't he say you could talk, just not about the case?" Ingrid said.

"'Cause," said Joey, with a little laugh. "Here we are talking about the case."

Ingrid laughed too – not much, but she couldn't help it. If only—

"Gotta go," Joey said suddenly.

"He's there?"

Click.

Call him back? Out of the question. Besides, she could hear the front door opening, people coming in.

"Hi," Mom called. "Anyone home?"

"Me," said Ingrid.

"Come see Grampy," Mom said.

Ingrid ran to the front hall. There were Mom, Dad, and Grampy; Grampy with a suitcase, that same suitcase she'd seen in his kitchen, looking around like he didn't know quite where he was.

"Grampy." She just kept going, into his arms.

Grampy patted her back. "Hiya, kid," he said. He was trembling, very slightly, but she could feel it. And his voice sounded thinner than usual, as though not all the vocal cords were working. "Hey," he said. "No crying in battle."

She stopped.

Mom took Grampy upstairs. Dad stood by the sink, rubbing his eyes. "Grampy's staying here?" Ingrid said.

"One of the conditions of his bail," Dad said.

"Was it really five hundred thousand dollars?"

"Not actual cash," Dad said. "We don't have five hundred thousand dollars in actual cash, in case you're under any illusions about that." Dad's look softened. "Sorry, Ingrid. This is a stressful time."

She nodded.

"We just had to sign a note, backed by the farm."

"Grampy could lose the farm?"

"Only by jumping bail – and that won't happen."

"Mr. Tulkinghorn's going to get him off, right, Dad?"

"It may not even come to trial," Dad said.

"You mean they'll drop the charges?"

"Snowball's chance," Dad said. "But Tulkinghorn, and don't breathe a word of this, wants—" Dad stopped himself. "You haven't been talking to Joey, have you?"

"Hardly at all."

"I don't want you talking to him."

"But what if we just don't discuss—"

"You heard me," Dad said.

Ingrid nodded. "What am I supposed to not breathe a word about?"

Dad lowered his voice. "Tulkinghorn's thinking of making a deal."

"What kind of deal?"

"Having Grampy plead guilty to a lesser charge," Dad said. "Avoiding a trial."

"What lesser charge?"

"Manslaughter," Dad said.

Ingrid had heard that word lots of times, but besides

the fact that it sounded horrible, like a kind of butchery, what did it really mean? "That's less than murder?" she said.

"Because of lack of intent or premeditation," Dad said. "Something that happens in the heat of the moment."

Lack of intent? Mr. Thatcher got shot from behind and from a long distance. But maybe none of that mattered if— "Dad? Would a deal mean Grampy goes free?"

"No way," Dad said. "Just that the sentence wouldn't be as long."

"But Dad. He's almost seventy-nine."

"I'm aware of that."

"And he didn't do it."

Dad gazed down at her.

"You know that, Dad, don't you? Grampy couldn't do a thing like—"

"Doesn't matter what I think," Dad said. "The problem's going to be getting Grampy to agree to a deal if Tulkinghorn can work one out."

"But why should he plead guilty to something he didn't do?"

"Even if that's true—"

"If?" said Ingrid. "If?"

"Let me finish," Dad said. "Try to imagine what Grampy would look like to a jury."

"Like a—" She was about to say *hero*, but Dad interrupted.

"Especially if the prosecutor pressed one of his buttons," Dad said. "One of his many buttons."

Ingrid said nothing. She could picture that scenario, way too clearly.

Dad checked his watch, frowned. "Got to go to the office for a few minutes," he said. "Be back soon."

Mom came downstairs. "Grampy might like some tea."

"I'll make it," Ingrid said. "Want some?"

"Thanks," Mom said. "Where's Dad?"

"Had to go in to the office."

"The office?"

"He said he'd be back soon."

"That's funny," Mom said. She stood there for a moment, an empty cup in her hand.

Ingrid took tea upstairs to Grampy. He was staying in the old spare bedroom, now Dad and Mom's home office. She found him sitting on the cot jammed between Dad's desk and the wall, staring at nothing. Light from the streetlamp came through the window, shading his skin and hair a sickly kind of yellow.

"Here's some tea, Grampy."

He took a sip. "Ah," he said. "That's more like it."

Ingrid went to the window, started closing the curtains. A car went by, passed under the streetlight: green hatchback. Ingrid recognized Mrs. McGreevy, hunched over the wheel. She closed the curtains. Grampy looked normal again, or almost. Ingrid had a sudden thought.

"What about Piggy?" she said.

"All set," Grampy said.

"Someone's taking care of him?"

"Yup," said Grampy. "And anyway, I intend to be back there soon."

"Really, Grampy? Are they going to let—"

"One way or another," he said.

"Oh," said Ingrid, trying to think how to steer him away from that idea. She sat beside him. "Who's taking care of Piggy?"

"Someone."

"Bob Borum?"

"Bob Borum?" said Grampy. "How do you know about him?"

"Isn't he a neighbor?"

"Yup."

"What's he like?"

"Got nothing against Bob Borum," said Grampy. "Used to run a dairy farm, second-last farm in Echo Falls."

"What does he do now?"

"Bob Borum? Owns that ice cream place."

"Not Moo Cow?" Moo Cow had the best ice cream in Echo Falls, possibly in the whole state.

"Yup," said Grampy.

Ingrid thought of her three-item list. She could try asking him where he was at the time of the murder. Or about what had happened to his Springfield .30-06 with the sniper scope. She glanced at Grampy's face. Bob Borum and the anonymous tip seemed a safer place to start. "How about we go there?" she said.

"Where?"

"Moo Cow."

"Ice cream in winter?" Grampy said. "I'll wait till spring."

That last sentence – *I'll wait till spring* – sparked a bad thought in Ingrid's mind: What if Grampy was locked up in the spring, living in some horrible cell, dangerous inmates all around? Unbearable. The most important item on the list, by far, was the second one, because the answer could make this all go away in a flash. She had to ask, no matter what. Ingrid took a deep breath, looked him in the eye.

"Grampy?" she said.

"Yeah?" he said, maybe sensing something because his eyes started to narrow.

Ingrid plunged on. "Where were you when Mr. Thatcher got killed?"

Now Grampy's eyes were slits. He gazed at her in a way he never had, a way she never wanted to see again. "You too?" he said.

"Oh, no," said Ingrid. "I know you could never do a thing like that. But why won't you just say? Then all this will—"

Grampy rose, a sudden movement that startled her. Tea slopped out of his mug and onto his hand, hot tea but he didn't seem to notice. "Because it's nobody's business," he said. "Period."

A fresh thought came to her, maybe one she should have had already, and she pressed on, defying that scary look in his eyes. "Are you protecting somebody, Grampy?"

"Don't give up, do you?" he said. "Get this straight – there's nobody I'd do that for." He paused, and when he continued, his voice was gentler. "Well, maybe one."

"Who?" said Ingrid, right away remembering Dad's

guilty face when the chief asked where he was at the time of the murder.

"Irrelevant," said Grampy. "She didn't do it."

twelve

were people at school looking at her funny? Ingrid couldn't tell. Ms. Groome was looking at her funny for sure, but nothing new there.

"And now, class," said Ms. Groome, "we've got just enough time for a quick pop quiz. Pass these around."

Ms. Groome had a thing for pop quizzes. This one – with the heading *Algebra Two Pop Quiz #46* – had seven questions, which should have been a good omen, but Ingrid knew better. She scanned the first one: *Two rafts are floating down the Mississippi River. The first raft travels at a speed of...*

Floating down the Mississippi River. That sounded pretty good right now. Ingrid had never seen the Mississippi River. Never even seen it, and yet she'd spent whole years of her life inside this school building, Ferrand Middle, where the air got so stuffy and overheated on winter afternoons like this. Nothing to be done about it – that was the way things were. But why? Did it have anything to do with those huge economic forces Dad sometimes talked about? *Like surfers on a wave – we can change our own direction a little bit but we can't change the wave.*

In the margin of Pop Quiz #46 Ingrid started sketching a surfer on a wave. Where to begin? How about the surfer's legs? Surfing must be all about balance, so maybe an angling calf line like so, and then another one, narrowing down to—

"Class. Pencils down. Pass your papers forward."

Yikes. Ingrid whipped through the answer boxes, filling in numbers willy-nilly.

"I see that 'pencils down' doesn't apply to you, Bruce. Mind telling the class what makes you so special?"

Everyone waited in anticipation. This was going to be good. Thank God for Brucie. Ingrid erased the beginnings of the surfer on her wave and passed in her quiz.

After school Ingrid handed in her bus permission slip, signed by Mom, allowing her to take bus 5, which went right past Moo Cow, instead of Mr. Sidney's, bus 2.

"No problem," Mom had said. "Who's going?"

"Just me," Ingrid said.

Mom gave her a long look. "Feel like a little treat?"

"Yeah." When wasn't that true?

"Okay," Mom said. "I'll pick you up."

When Ingrid got on the bus, she found herself sitting across from the Dratch twins. Their big heads turned to her as one.

"Hey," said Dwayne.

"You're on the wrong bus," said Dustin.

"Yeah," said Dwayne. "The wrong bus."

Ingrid held up the bus pass, gave them her best expressionless look. The Dratch twins squinted at the bus pass as though trying to crack some code. Then they went back to doing what they'd been doing, which meant sitting slack faced in their usual catatonic way. The bus was on Main Street, only a couple blocks before Moo Cow, when Dwayne suddenly came to life.

"Hey," he said, turning to Ingrid again. "Hill."

"Hill?" said Dustin.

"Yeah," said Dwayne. "It's her grandpop."

"The—" Dustin said.

Dwayne made his hand into a gun and fired at Ingrid. "Grand*pop*," he said. "Get it? *Pop pop pop.*"

Dwayne Dratch was huge, like a full-grown man. Ingrid had weighed ninety-seven pounds at her annual checkup last month. She didn't think about any of that, didn't think at all, just smacked Dwayne's hand away.

Dwayne gazed at his hand in disbelief. Dustin gazed at Dwayne's hand in disbelief. Dwayne and Dustin gazed at each other. Their faces got bright red. Both red faces started turning toward Ingrid, again as one.

"Moo Cow," said the driver, stopping the bus. Ingrid made her way to the front, trying not to hurry. She felt eyes on her, looking at her funny, no question about it. *"Pop pop,"* said someone, not a Dratch, as Ingrid got off the bus.

Moo Cow, a restored old country store, had a bell that went *tinkle-tinkle* when you opened the door. Then came the smell of chocolate rising from the cauldron behind the deeply polished wooden counter on the candy side of the store, heavenly. No customers, no one around but the skinny guy with the long gray ponytail, the only worker Ingrid had ever seen in Moo Cow. He was over on the ice cream side, weighing a mound of jujubes – they looked like jewels – on a brass scale.

"Hi," he said. "Peanut almond mocha swirl?"

"Thanks," Ingrid said. The ponytail guy was great at remembering what the kids liked.

"Small, medium, or large?"

Ingrid shrugged off her backpack, opened the Velcro pocket: two ones, three quarters, six nickels, and a penny.

"Small."

"Cup or cone?"

"Cup."

"Toppings?"

"Jimmies."

"Two ninety-five."

Leaving her with eleven cents: She knew Moo Cow.

But for some reason, she'd never paid much attention to the ponytail guy. The ponytail guy got busy with his scoop. He was skinny, but his hands were thick and strong, with big green veins – kind of like Grampy's: the hands of a man who'd done a lot of hard work. He sprinkled on the jimmies and slid the cup of peanut almond mocha swirl across the counter.

"Thanks," said Ingrid, and after a pause took a chance and added, "Mr. Borum."

He raised an eyebrow. "You have the advantage of me," he said. Ingrid had no clue what that meant. Maybe he read that on her face. "Meaning," he said,

"I don't believe I know *your* name."

"Ingrid," said Ingrid. "We talked on the phone once."

"We did?"

"When I answered at my grandfather's place last fall."

"And your grandfather would be...?"

"Aylmer Hill."

"Ah." He opened the cash register, put the $2.95 inside. "And ... and how is he?"

"Okay," Ingrid said. "He's with us right now."

"Out on...?"

"Yes," said Ingrid. "He says you had the second-last farm in Echo Falls."

"True," said Mr. Borum. He gazed at Ingrid for a moment. "I'd like your opinion on something."

"What's that?"

Mr. Borum opened a freezer door behind him, took out a plastic mixing bowl. "I've been fooling around with a new flavor," he said, dipping a spoon into the bowl and handing it to her. "What do you think?"

A strange-looking ice cream: red, orange, and yellow, like lava from a volcano. Ingrid lowered the spoon without tasting. "You called about hearing a boom," she said.

"And you told me there was no boom."

Ingrid nodded.

"But that must have been dynamite I heard," Mr. Borum said.

"Yes."

"Mind telling me what was going on?"

"You first," Ingrid said. Had she really said that? It shocked her – so rude, and Mr. Borum seemed so nice. But Grampy was in big trouble, accused of a murder he hadn't done; that meant getting behind how things seemed to how they actually were.

Mr. Borum looked taken aback. "Me first what?"

Too late to stop now. "Someone made an anonymous call to Mr. Thatcher," Ingrid said.

"So I read in *The Echo*," said Mr. Borum. "For what that's worth." He blinked. "Oh my God – Aylmer thinks it was me?"

Ingrid didn't actually know what Grampy thought about that, or if he'd even thought about it at all, so she didn't answer.

"I've always liked Aylmer," said Mr. Borum. "We both did." He paused for a moment, tilted his head slightly, as though trying to see Ingrid from a different angle, and said, "My partner and I. When he died, I sold off the herd and most of the land – too much work for one man. You know what your grandfather did before that happened?"

"No."

"Offered to take over the morning milking, no charge."

"He did?"

"Aylmer didn't want me to lose" – Mr. Borum's eyes got a little liquid – "everything. So I would never – ever – do anything to harm him. Please make sure he knows that."

"Okay," Ingrid said. She took a breath and plunged on. "Who bought your land?"

Something about the question made Mr. Borum smile. He had nice teeth, white and even. "You even look a little like him," he said.

"Who?"

"Aylmer."

"My grandfather bought your land?"

"No, no," said Mr. Borum. "Some company, can't even remember the name. But it was controlled by the Ferrands."

Suspicion confirmed. "What are they going to do with it?" Ingrid said.

"Whatever they can get away with," said Mr. Borum. "But that sample's getting soft, and I'm still waiting for your expert opinion."

Ingrid tasted the new flavor. "Wow," she said.

"Yeah?" said Mr. Borum, looking pleased. "Think it'll sell?"

"Lots," said Ingrid. She licked the spoon.

"Needs a name," Mr. Borum said.

"How about Lava?" Ingrid said.

Mr. Borum shook his head. "Not enough pizzazz." He thought for a moment and said, "I've got it – Ingrid's Special!"

"Really?"

He turned and wrote at the bottom of the chalkboard: !!NEW!! INGRID'S SPECIAL!!!

Mr. Borum went over to the candy side, stirred the chocolate. Ingrid ate her peanut almond mocha swirl, no longer her favorite; it didn't compare to Ingrid's Special.

"So," said Mr. Borum, dipping his finger into the cauldron for a little taste – was this a dream job or what? – "tell me about the dynamiting."

Ingrid told the story: sinkhole, four sticks, endangered toad eggs. Mr. Borum was silent for a moment, then laughed and laughed.

"That Aylmer," he said. "He's got a genius for making trouble."

Ingrid stopped eating her ice cream. "But he's *in* trouble now," she said.

Mr. Borum nodded.

"Grampy could never do what they're saying," Ingrid said.

Mr. Borum spoke gently. "He does have a temper, Ingrid. And he's not fond of government interference. Or any interference at all, for that matter."

"Mr. Thatcher was shot from behind," Ingrid said. "And from a long distance."

"I see what you're saying," said Mr. Borum. "But if he didn't do it, why isn't he talking?"

"I don't know." That was the most important question, of course, although she'd forgotten to put it on her list. There was so much she didn't know, and every passing day brought Grampy's trial closer. She thought of something Holmes had said impatiently to Dr. Watson in "The Adventure of the Copper Beeches," one of her favorites: "Data! data! data! I can't make bricks without clay." She needed data. Data were facts, such as the identity of the anonymous tipster who'd ratted out Grampy about the dynamiting episode. Why not start there? "Someone made that anonymous call," she said.

"True," said Mr. Borum.

"But you can't even see the road from that sinkhole," Ingrid said. "Or any buildings, not even Grampy's." Except for that little shed.

"So you're saying...?"

"Someone must have been watching." But from where? "Maybe from the orchard. Or even behind the shed."

"Behind the shed?" said Mr. Borum.

"Yes, there's this shed at the top of—" Ingrid began, but she stopped herself. There was something on Mr. Borum's mind.

"I know that shed," he said. "I've got one – I had one – very like it. Odd."

"What's odd?"

"Doubt it means anything at all," said Mr. Borum, "but one night – not too long before I made up my mind to sell out – I caught a prowler snooping around down there, around my shed."

"What kind of prowler?" Ingrid said.

"Hard to say. I only got a glimpse of him in my flash-light beam before he ran away. Looked like a hobo, maybe searching for a dry place to bed down for the night."

"Looked like a hobo?" Ingrid said.

"With long greasy hair. Blond."

"Blond?"

Mr. Borum nodded. "Kind of creepy, too. In retro-spect, maybe a little too well fed for an actual hobo, kind of fat faced. But why all these questions, Ingrid? Are you on to something?"

Before Ingrid could reply, the bell went *tinkle-tinkle*. The door opened and a tall man wearing an eye patch entered: Major Ferrand. A woman – Ingrid saw that she'd been holding the door for him – followed Major Ferrand inside. She had a hawk nose and wild white hair, streaked with black.

"Welcome," said Mr. Borum, wiping his hands on his apron. "The usual?"

Major Ferrand ignored him; the woman gave a curt nod. Neither took the slightest notice of Ingrid. They sat at a table facing each other, not speaking. Mr. Borum made two espressos, carried them over, also bringing a cup of Ingrid's Special and two spoons.

"We didn't order ice cream," said Major Ferrand.

"Free sample of our latest concoction," said Mr. Borum. "Ingrid's Special."

Major Ferrand frowned. "Ingrid?" he said.

Mr. Borum turned toward Ingrid and smiled. Major Ferrand and the woman followed his gaze. Did Major Ferrand recognize her? Ingrid wasn't sure. His frown deepened, and he said, "No ice cream," pushing the cup away with the back of his hand.

Mr. Borum's smile faded a little. He backed away. The hawk-nosed woman took up a spoon and dipped it in the cup. Just as she was putting the ice cream in her mouth, Major Ferrand leaned forward and whispered to her. The woman made a horrible face, as though she'd tasted rotten fish, and spat the sample of Ingrid's Special into her napkin.

Mr. Borum looked alarmed. He hurried to their table.

"It does not agree with me," said the woman.

"I'm sorry," said Mr. Borum.

"Check," said Major Ferrand.

thirteen

data! data! data!

Ingrid awoke in the night, sat up with a jerk. She switched on the reading light. *The Complete Sherlock Holmes* lay in its usual place on the bedside table. She opened it to "A Case of Identity", leafed through to a passage she'd highlighted: *You did not know where to look, and so you missed all that was important. I can never bring you to realize the importance of sleeves, the suggestiveness of thumbnails, or the great issues that may hang from a bootlace.*

Yes, that was her, missing everything that was important. She went over her list: Who was the anonymous tipster? Where was Grampy? Where was the murder weapon? Add to that Bob Borum's question: Why wouldn't Grampy say where he was at the time of the murder? Those four questions buzzed around in her brain, bouncing off one another, refusing to add up to anything, just zooming faster and faster.

Ingrid turned the pages to "The Five Orange Pips",

a strange story that ended up being about the Ku Klux Klan, and stopped at another highlighted passage: *The ideal reasoner would, when he had once been shown a single fact in all its bearings, deduce from it not only all the chain of events which led up to it but also all the results which would follow from it.*

She read it over three times, began to suspect she was a bad deducer. For example, she'd already deduced that the anonymous tipster was the murderer. But what sense did that make? Wasn't the tipster trying to make trouble for Grampy? Then why kill off Mr. Thatcher, the guy who was going to make the actual trouble? What was the expression? Cat's-paw? Yeah. Why kill off the cat's-paw? Made no sense. So maybe she should erase the tipster question – one of those red herrings – from the list. *Cat's-paw* and *red herring*, coming so close together, somehow made her feel a little nauseated, one of those weird things that could happen when anybody with any brains was fast asleep.

Ingrid closed the book, switched off the light, shut her eyes. But they popped right back open. Why? Because Mr. Borum's creepy prowler sounded a lot like the guy who'd snapped her picture from that car with the mudded-out license plate. And therefore? She had no clue.

From down the hall, in the direction of the office, came the sound of coughing. Not loud, maybe muffled by a hand, but it went on for a pretty long time. After that, silence. Seas rose in Ingrid's mind, and her sturdy little boat took shape. She was almost asleep when the coughing started up again.

*   *   *

"Imagine," said Jill Monteiro, "that you're walking through a dark, dark forest. We've got a lot of good stuff left over from *Macbeth*" – a disastrous production from the year before Ingrid joined the Prescott Players, Meredith O'Malley's out-damned-spot speech ending in a fit of giggles that people still talked about – "and I know Mr. Rubino will come up with scary lighting effects."

Ingrid and Brucie walked across the stage.

"Brucie?" said Jill. "Is that you whistling?"

He nodded vigorously, kept whistling.

"And your thinking?"

"Whistling in the dark," said Brucie. "Ever heard that expression?"

"I have," said Jill. "But wasn't that 'Yankee Doodle Dandy'?"

"So?"

"I'm not sure 'Yankee Doodle Dandy' fits the mood," said Jill. "Silence, building tension – that's what we're about in this scene."

"But—"

In a very low voice, Ingrid, stealing a line from Mr. Sidney, said, "Zip it."

Brucie's eyes widened. He zipped it. The rehearsal went smoothly after that. Ingrid lost herself totally in Gretel's fear. Today, for some reason, she could do fear effortlessly.

On the way out, Jill said, "You were great today."

Ingrid felt herself beaming.

Jill put her hand on Ingrid's shoulder. "Holding up?"

Ingrid nodded. Jill was about to say something else when Brucie sidled up.

"Got a question, Bruce?"

"Yeah," said Brucie. "Who's your agent?"

Jill turned a little pink. "Why do you ask?"

"Thought maybe it was time."

"Time?"

"For me to get one too."

"I'll tell you when," said Jill.

Mom drove Ingrid home.

"Any news?" Ingrid said.

"No." Mom bit her lip almost the whole way.

The Echo lay in the driveway. Ingrid brought it into the kitchen. Ty was at the table, working his way through a family-size package of potato chips, the garlic-and-onion-flavored kind, inedible in Ingrid's opinion.

"You'll spoil your dinner," Mom said.

Ty answered with his mouth full, incomprehensible.

Ingrid took *The Echo* from its wrapper, and there, below the fold, saw a photo of a man she recognized, a man with an eye patch. MEET CYRUS FERRAND, read the headline; and the subheads: THE WORLD WAR II BOYS FROM ECHO FALLS and FIRST IN A SERIES.

"Where's Grampy?"

Ty, at the fridge, drinking OJ from the carton – a big no-no, but Mom, putting something in the oven, didn't notice – said, "Playing with Nigel."

"He's playing with Nigel?"

"Out back."

Ingrid went out back, *The Echo* in her hand. The

outdoor lights were on, illuminating Grampy and Nigel against a backdrop of the woods, already dark, and the evening sky above, still streaked with purple. Grampy didn't notice her. He threw a tennis ball toward the woods and said, "Git."

Like that was going to happen. Nigel had no retrieving ability whatsoever, had never once brought back any object thrown for him. Instead, he'd just gaze into the distance, sometimes in the direction of the ball or whatever it was and sometimes not, until—

But what was this? Nigel was on his feet, actually headed toward the tennis ball, lodged at the base of the nearest tree – quite a long throw.

"Dillydallying," said Grampy. "Pick up the pace."

Ingrid almost laughed out loud. Pick up the pace: as if Nigel—

But Nigel began to run; not that ridiculous waddling drunken-sailor thing, but a real straight-line run, and far from slow. He grabbed the ball in one motion, no fumbling, and came running back.

"Sit," said Grampy.

Nigel sat.

"Give it up," said Grampy.

Nigel dropped the ball at Grampy's feet.

"Not like that," Grampy said.

Nigel picked up the ball, held it loosely in his mouth for Grampy to take it. Grampy took it.

"Lotta work to do," he said. He patted Nigel on the head, one quick pat, over and gone.

Nigel wagged his tail, harder than Ingrid had ever seen him.

"Grampy?"

He turned. For a moment he looked so full of life, all rosy and having fun. Then it faded.

"How did you get Nigel to do that?"

"Do what?" Grampy said.

"Retrieve."

"It's in his genes."

"It is?"

"Sure. He's half Lab, maybe more."

"Nigel?" Nigel looked nothing like a Lab to Ingrid.

"But the rest of him's trash," said Grampy. "What you got there?"

"*The Echo*," she said, holding it out.

"That rag?" said Grampy. "Wouldn't waste my time."

"Yeah, but look – the World War Two series has started."

He took the paper, gazed hard at Cyrus Ferrand's picture. His eyes went back and forth, back and forth, got harder and harder. He came to the end of the article and threw the paper in the snow.

"Grampy – what's wrong?"

Grampy didn't answer. He walked to the house. Nigel trotted after him, but Grampy didn't notice. He closed the door in Nigel's face.

Ingrid picked up the paper, smoothed it out.

MEET CYRUS FERRAND
THE WORLD WAR II BOYS FROM ECHO FALLS
FIRST IN A SERIES
ANOTHER ECHO EXCLUSIVE

"It was a war for survival," says Cyrus Ferrand. "We all did our duty."

Major Ferrand is one of those John Wayne-style heroes who don't like to talk much about themselves. Now resident in the Caribbean, but Echo Falls born and bred, he is one of five surviving men of our town who went off to fight in World War II. Three of them – Myron Sidney, Major Ferrand, and Aylmer Hill – were all on Corregidor, a strategically important island off Manila in the Philippines, when it was captured by the Japanese in May 1942.

"We put up a hell of a fight," says Major Ferrand, "but without air cover against the Japanese bombardment it was hopeless."

History buffs will remember that the surrender was just the beginning of the nightmare for the Corregidor survivors, who ended up on the notorious Bataan Death March. Even so long after the event, the Death March is not a subject Major Ferrand will talk about.

"Time is a great healer," he says.

How did the war change him? "We all grew up pretty fast," he says. He adds that lifelong friendships were formed, although he has not kept up with Mr. Sidney or Mr. Hill. Major Ferrand, a one-time racer on the ocean yacht circuit, describes himself as a "retired investor" and says he lives "very quietly now. It was all long ago."

Next week: Myron "Boom Boom" Sidney.

What had got Grampy so angry-looking, or if not anger, some other emotion that had made his eyes go so hard? Ingrid reread the article and couldn't come up with anything. She could almost hear the voice of Sherlock Holmes. *You did not know where to look.*

She went back inside. No one in the kitchen but Nigel, lying by the water bowl in his usual splayed-out way. Ingrid gave him a long look. "What other tricks do you know?" she said.

No response.

"Ingrid," Mom called downstairs. "Can you run the laundry?"

"What about Ty?"

"I can't hear you."

"WHAT ABOUT TY?"

"He's out taking Nigel for a walk."

"No he's not."

"Can't hear you."

"NO HE'S NOT."

"He's not? TY! TY!"

Silence.

Ingrid went into the laundry room. Dirty clothes were piled high in the plastic hamper. She opened the washing machine. Also full of clothes, but these were all damp and twisted up, meaning first she had to throw them into the dryer. She opened the dryer. Oh, no. Full of clothes too, but all dry. If they'd been wet, she could

135

have just pressed the start button and called it a day, standard 99 Maple Lane procedure in a backed-up-laundry situation. Now she had to empty the dryer, fold all the jeans, shirts, T-shirts, skirts, pair up the socks, lay everything neatly in hamper two. After that came tossing the damp clothes from washer to dryer, and only then, what seemed like an hour later, could she actually "run the laundry," which probably sounded like nothing to a beginner, more play than work.

Ingrid was no beginner. Was there anything more tedious than this? The same repetitive thing, over and over, the only difference being that for the first time, some of the clothes were Grampy's. Like Dad and Ty, Grampy wore boxers, not briefs. Was that a family thing? She found herself wondering what Joey wore. Her mind wandered a bit after that, and she almost missed something in the chest pocket of one of Grampy's shirts. A mistake like that could mean laundry-room disaster. Once Dad's fountain pen had somehow slipped by and—

What was this thing anyway? Some kind of ticket stub? She removed it from Grampy's pocket. Not the long skinny ball-game kind or the tiny movie kind: this stub, red and black, was for parking. At the top it said, *New York City Mercy Hospital.*

Ingrid slipped it into her own pocket. A very strange moment in the laundry room – now she really could hear Holmes, as though he were there, speaking in Basil Rathbone's voice. *I can never bring you to realize the importance of sleeves, the suggestiveness of thumbnails, or the great issues that may hang from a bootlace.*

Why couldn't she be smarter? She needed to be smarter, and fast.

fourteen

data. It could come in the form of information, things you heard and saw. For example, take the creepy-looking guy who'd snapped her picture, or maybe hers and Nigel's. Mr. Borum had seen a prowler matching that description around his shed, back when he'd still owned the dairy farm. Were those two links in a chain? If so, it was hard not to connect them to Grampy's shed, a perfect spot for watching the dynamite caper without being seen. Was that a third link, a third link in a chain that led to the identity of the anonymous tipster? Ingrid couldn't prove it, but she knew. That mudded-out license plate might as well have read: GUILTY.

Data could also be an object, like the parking stub she'd found in Grampy's shirt. Sherlock Holmes was great at seeing big meanings in little things. Take how he knew from some scratches on Watson's shoe in "A Scandal in Bohemia" both that Watson had been getting himself very wet lately and that he had a careless servant girl. Little things with big meanings: alone in her room that night, the house quiet, Ingrid examined the parking stub under her desk lamp.

The parking stub was square, about two inches by two inches, with perforations at the bottom where the end had been torn off. *New York City Mercy Hospital* was printed in white letters at the top. Then came an address: 23 East End Avenue. After that, in tiny print, were lots of parking garage rules. Ingrid made her way through them all. They mostly added up to the garage not being responsible for anything. What would Holmes have seen? Ingrid didn't know.

She flipped the stub over. On the back was a map of East End Avenue and surrounding streets; Ingrid saw that the East River flowed nearby. Putting that together with memories of her two trips to New York, she felt pretty sure that New York Mercy Hospital was on the Upper East Side of Manhattan. What else? She stared at the back of the stub. There was an inky smear in the middle, hard to read, as though the printer had been jolted or something. Not exactly a printer – maybe more like a stamper. Yes, one of those stamping machines they had in parking garages. You stuck the ticket in the machine on the way into the garage, then gave it to the clerk on the way out, and the clerk stamped it and told you the amount. And therefore...

Ingrid bent over Grampy's parking stub, squinted at the blurry print. In: 11:05 a.m., Tue., Feb. 11. Out: 10:17 a.m., Sat., Feb. 15.

Sat., Feb. 15? She turned to her computer, brought up the calendar, double-checked. Yes: the day she and Joey had snowshoed on the old Indian trail, ended up finding the body of Harris Thatcher. And Grampy? He hadn't been home at first, but then had appeared in dress pants, his suitcase in the kitchen. So that added up. But way more important than that was Tue., Feb. 11. Ingrid's heart started beating very fast, like she'd been running a long race. Tue., Feb. 11 was the day of Mr. Thatcher's murder, according to the medical examiner. When, exactly? Ingrid couldn't remember. She went to *The Echo*'s site – a dinky little site with a shaky video of the falls – and found the article: *between noon and 3:00 P.M.*

Grampy, or someone with the parking ticket, had checked into a New York City parking garage at 11:05, fifty-five minutes before the beginning of the medical examiner's time period. Grampy, or that someone, had been hundreds of miles away on the day of the murder.

Maybe not hundreds. Ingrid went to MapQuest, checked the distance from Echo Falls to New York City Mercy Hospital: 112 miles. How long did it take to drive 112 miles? A couple hours, probably, maybe more in heavy traffic. She tried to imagine ways the ticket holder could have parked in the hospital garage, hurried back to Echo Falls by some other means of transport in time to kill Mr. Thatcher before 3:00 p.m., then return to New York and have the ticket stamped out on Saturday. More like the kind of thing that happened in second-rate movies, but possible. Possible if you were really clever at being sneaky. Not Grampy.

And therefore? Therefore right in the palm of her hand she was holding evidence – hard and unshakable – of Grampy's innocence. She jumped up, on her way to spread the news, to shout it through the whole house. But at her door she paused. Grampy knew he was innocent. Even if he'd somehow forgotten the parking stub, there were probably lots of ways he could prove he'd been in New York at the time of the murder. He hadn't done so. Why not? Was it conceivable he'd engineered some second-rate movie scheme after all? Ingrid remembered one of Holmes's most important sayings, from *The Sign of Four*: *When you have eliminated the impossible, whatever remains,* however improbable, *must be the truth.*

So where was she? Ingrid wasn't sure. She wavered at the door. Another question lurked in the background, maybe the biggest: What was Grampy doing at New York City Mercy Hospital in the first place? Ingrid moved back into her room. She slid the parking stub into an envelope and stuck it under some papers in her top desk drawer.

The next morning it was snowing, not hard but maybe enough. Ingrid switched on Roxy 101, caught the school closings. Glastonbury closed, Windsor closed, Cheshire two-hour delay, South Harrow closed, Simsbury closed, Echo Falls open. Echo Falls open? She couldn't have heard right.

Ty was in the bathroom; Ingrid knew from the sound of water splashing all over the place. She knocked on the door.

"Ty? Is there school?"

"Why else would I be up, you moron?"

*   *   *

The bus was late. Big surprise. All over central Connecticut kids were tucked safe and sound in their beds. Only in Echo Falls, for some reason, were they expected—

Ingrid saw Mia outside her house a couple blocks away, a tiny figure behind a snowflake curtain. She walked up the street. Mia was facing the other way, didn't see her.

"Hi," Ingrid called.

Mia jumped; not a jump, maybe more like she'd been jolted by electricity. She turned. "Oh my God. You scared me."

Ingrid raised her hands like claws, made a monster face. Then she noticed how pale Mia's own face was; plus red-rimmed eyes and dark circles under them. "Something wrong?" she said.

Mia's eyes met Ingrid's, then shifted away. She looked almost embarrassed about something, but what sense did that make? Ingrid was trying to think of what to say next when Mia's face crumpled and she burst into tears.

"Mia?"

"Oh, Ingrid." Mia stumbled forward, bumped against Ingrid, almost falling. Ingrid held her.

"What is it?"

"This is my last day."

"Your last day?" Ingrid felt Mia's tears on her own face.

"I'm going back to New York," Mia said. "To live with my father."

"Today?"

"He'll be here after school."

"But why?"

Mia sobbed, shaking in Ingrid's arms. "I'm so sorry," she said. "You're the best friend I'll ever have."

"But why now, in the middle of the school year?" Ingrid said.

"That part's okay," Mia said through her tears. "I'm going back to my old school." She kept crying.

"We'll still be friends," Ingrid said, her own voice choking up. "And there's nothing to be sorry about. I just don't understand why."

Mia backed away, wiping her face on the sleeve of her jacket. "Oh, God, Ingrid."

"Oh, God, what?"

But Mia just shook her head. The bus appeared, coming slowly down Maple Lane. Mia's eyes widened. "Do I look like I've been crying?"

"No," Ingrid said. A total lie. "Don't worry – it's only one hundred and twelve miles."

"What is?"

"From here to the east side of Manhattan."

The bus pulled up. "That's where my dad lives," Mia said.

"Perfect," said Ingrid.

Mia laughed, just a little bit. "How do you know the mileage?"

The door opened. "Morning, petunias," said Mr. Sidney.

Being at school on what should have been a snow day made everyone grumpy, teachers too. All except Mr. Porterhouse in gym, who was practically bouncing up and down with positive energy.

"Let's shoot some hoops," he said. "Two half courts, five on five, subs rotate in, captains Stacy, Carlos, Matt, and Anna, choose 'em up, boy girl boy girl, let's go."

Ingrid ended up on Carlos's team, third pick, which was just about right. Basketball was not her sport: that ball, so huge and unmanageable, and the hoop so high. But she loved running, and there was lots of that. Whenever the ball came her way, she passed it immediately to Carlos and he took care of the rest. Carlos was probably the best athlete in the school – Ty said the Red Raiders football coach already knew about him – and made the game seem easy. Like right now, the way he dribbled around Joey, Anna's first pick, like he wasn't there, and went in for an easy layup, almost touching the rim. After that he came racing back on defense, said, "Nice pass, Ingrid," then stripped the ball from Joey and passed it to her. She passed it right back the way she always did, and Carlos somehow dribbled the ball through Dustin Dratch's legs and took it in for another easy two.

"Nice pass, Ingrid," he said, backpedaling up the court faster than most of the others could run forward. "You're first pick next time."

Joey came dribbling up the court, his chin stuck way out. Carlos glided over to cover him. Joey crashed into Carlos, and they both went down. Mr. Porterhouse blew the whistle.

"On you, Joey. That's a charge. He had position."

Joey looked real mad all of a sudden, his face red and swollen in a way Ingrid had never seen. "No, he didn't."

Mr. Porterhouse blew the whistle again. "That's a technical. Shooting two, Carlos."

Carlos made them both, of course. His team ended up drubbing all the others. That meant each player won a prize; the prizes were always baseball cards from Mr. Porterhouse's collection. Ingrid got Rich "El Guapo" Garces.

On the way out of the gym she felt a tap on her shoulder. She turned: Joey, face still red. In a low voice, almost a whisper, he said, "Soon I can talk to you again. Like normal."

"Why?" said Ingrid.

"Um," said Joey. "Uh." His mouth opened and closed, opened again. But before he could say anything more, Carlos came loping by.

"Way to go, Ingrid," he said. "Who'd you get?"

Ingrid showed him her card. Carlos laughed.

"What's funny?" said Ingrid.

"*El Guapo* means 'the handsome one'," said Carlos.

Ingrid checked the card again and laughed too. Carlos zoomed away. Ingrid looked around for Joey, but he was gone, so she couldn't ask him why they could soon be talking normally. Even if Grampy won the trial, it wouldn't be soon, might be months away. So what was up?

After school Ingrid had rehearsal. Meredith O'Malley's mother, a seamstress, handled costumes. The cast tried them on.

"I'm not wearing these itty-bitty shorts," Brucie said.

"They're genuine lederhosen," said Mrs. O'Malley. "I copied them from a real German catalogue."

"*Achtung,*" said Brucie.

"What does that mean?" said Mrs. O'Malley.

"No way," said Brucie.

But Ingrid's dress was kind of cute.

Dad drove her home. He gave her a big smile.

"How was rehearsal?"

"Good."

"Play coming along okay?"

"I think so."

"Can't wait to see it."

"Yeah?"

"Of course," Dad said. "Not a big fan of theater, I'll admit, but I'm a big fan of yours."

Hey. That was nice. Ingrid gave Dad a smile back. He looked more relaxed than he'd been recently, wore a beautiful light-blue shirt; still the handsomest dad in Echo Falls.

"Any news, Dad?" she said as they turned into Maple Lane.

"News?"

"About the case."

He glanced at her. "Too soon to talk about it."

"Too soon to talk about what?" Ingrid said. "Tell me. I can keep a secret."

"Can you?"

"I promise."

"Not a word till I give the okay?"

"Not a word."

Dad took a deep breath. Good news was coming;

Ingrid could feel it: that was why Dad was so much more like himself. "It looks like Grampy's going to take the deal," he said.

For a moment her brain refused to understand. "He's going to plead guilty to murder?"

"To manslaughter, as I told you already."

"And go to jail?"

"Not for too long."

"How long?"

"That's still being worked out. But it won't be more than six or seven years, assuming good behavior."

Six or seven years? "But that's a death sentence, Dad."

"Control yourself, Ingrid. It's Grampy's choice."

"But why? He didn't do it."

"For one thing," Dad said, "Mrs. Thatcher has agreed not to sue if Grampy cops a plea."

"Mrs. Thatcher?" Ingrid didn't get it at all.

"She's got health problems," Dad said. "Doesn't want to face a trial."

"But what if the jury said Grampy was innocent?"

"She could still sue for wrongful death," Dad said. "And according to Tulkinghorn, there's a very good chance she'd win. We – Grampy – would lose the farm."

"Oh, God," Ingrid said. It was so complicated, so hard. And Joey saying soon they could talk normally again? He knew the deal was in the works. Yes, hard and complicated.

A big black car was parked outside 99 Maple Lane.

Dad's headlights shone on the license plate: New York.

"Wonder who that is," Dad said, pulling into the driveway. They got out of the TT.

The big black car looked vaguely familiar. Ingrid saw someone sitting in the front. Hey. Mia. At that moment, on their way to the house, Dad a few steps ahead of Ingrid, the front door opened and a man came out. Ingrid recognized him: Mia's dad, Mr. McGreevy. He walked quickly by, not looking at them, got into the black car and drove away, tires squealing.

"Who the hell was that?" Dad said.

Then Mom appeared in the doorway, face lit by the outside light. She looked awful. "Mark," she said, in a voice that didn't sound like her at all, harsh and ragged, "is it true you're having an affair with Lisa McGreevy?"

fifteen

"**i** just hate him," Ty said.

Ingrid felt her face twisting up as though she were about to cry, but no tears came. She was all cried out. They were in Ty's room, maybe less than two hours after Mia's father's one and only visit to 99 Maple Lane, a visit that had changed everything. Even Ty's wall: there was a fist-size hole in the plaster now, and Ty's knuckles were bloody. Just in case Ingrid tried thinking that this was some nightmare she could awake from, that hole in the wall – so undeniable – was there to stop her.

Two hours that had begun in raging noise – Mom screaming, Dad screaming back, Mom saying words to Dad that Ingrid had never heard from her mouth, Dad banging out the door, suitcase in hand; and Grampy in the background, his skin colorless, his eyes, normally sky blue, suddenly dark, like the sky at night. Now the house was quiet: Mom in her room, door closed; Dad gone to the farm; Grampy around somewhere.

Any chance it wasn't true, that Mr. McGreevy was just

making trouble? Oh, he was making trouble, no doubt about that, but it had to be true. Dad hadn't denied it, for one thing. Mia had probably found out somehow – which was why she'd been acting so strange lately, why she was going to New York. Had Mr. McGreevy learned the secret from her? Or maybe, seeing her mood, wormed it out of her? At that moment Ingrid realized she herself had come close to finding out much earlier, down in that parking lot by the falls. Pretty obvious now who'd been sitting on the bench with Mrs. McGreevy – and now Ingrid also remembered those quick phone calls in the TT, and Dad's late trips back to the office, late trips that coincided twice with Ingrid's sightings of Mrs. McGreevy driving down the street in her green hatchback, face intense under the streetlamp. And one more thing: Dad's guilty face when Chief Strade asked him to account for his whereabouts at the time of the murder. Dad had an alibi, way too embarrassing to use. Had he ended up using it after all? Did the chief know?

"Mom's way prettier than that bitch," Ty said.

"I was thinking the same thing," Ingrid said.

"I didn't even know he knew her."

"Me neither." But at that moment Ingrid remembered that when Mia and her mother were still new to Echo Falls, a tree had fallen on their lawn and Dad had gone over with the chain saw. Could it have started way back then? She got a terrible inkling of the kinds of thoughts that must be whirling around in Mom's head.

There was a knock at the door.

"Yeah?" said Ty.

The door opened. Ingrid had expected Mom, but it

was Grampy. His skin was still pale, but his eyes were back to normal.

"You kids eaten?" he said.

They shook their heads.

"Gotta eat," he said.

"We're not hungry," Ty said.

"Makes no difference." Grampy reached into his pocket, handed them each a Slim Jim. They took the Slim Jims, peeled the tops off the wrappers. Grampy glanced at the hole in the wall, sat on the end of Ty's bed beside Ingrid. Ty was sitting up at the head of the bed, back against the pillows. The room wasn't big, and they were all close together, but for some reason it didn't feel crowded.

"Grampy?" Ingrid said. "What's going to happen?"

"Don't know."

"Divorce?" Ty said.

"Maybe," said Grampy. "Eat."

They each took a bite. It wasn't one of those times you realized you were hungry after all, at least not for Ingrid. She had to chew and chew to get that bite down.

"Gotta eat," Grampy said. "I've seen men die."

"Huh?" said Ty.

"But never mind that," Grampy said. "The point I'm making is you're both good kids. Strong kids. And much closer to being adults than babies, if you see what I mean."

Ingrid wasn't sure. Ty said, "If you're not gonna eat that..." He'd polished off his Slim Jim already. She handed him hers.

Grampy gave him a sharp look. "Counting on you, son," he said.

"To do what?"

"Be a man," Grampy said. After a pause, he added, "Or at least act your age."

Another pause, and then a funny thing happened: they all started laughing. Not loud, not long, but real laughing. At a time like this, with the family falling apart and Grampy on the way to pleading guilty to a crime he didn't commit, how could they be laughing? Ingrid didn't understand. But they were.

Grampy rose, his knees creaking, and patted Ingrid on the head.

"How could this happen, Grampy?"

Grampy replied, his eyes on Ty. "A man's got to do his thinking with his brain," he said.

Ingrid didn't get that either. The brain was what did the thinking: basic anatomy, no?

Next morning was the first school day in a long time that Ingrid got up before Mom had to wake her. She showered – signs in the bathroom that Ty had been there first – dressed, and went downstairs.

Mom, Ty, and Grampy were in the kitchen. Mom wore her nicest business suit, the gray flannel skirt and jacket. Her face was puffy, and she was wearing more makeup than usual, and where she'd missed with the makeup, her skin was like ashes, but she looked okay.

"Morning, Ingrid," she said.

"Hi, Mom. Hi, everybody."

Ty made some noise, his mouth full of French toast.

French toast? Wasn't that a weekend thing? Grampy, drinking coffee beside Ty, said, "Hi, kid."

They had a quick breakfast, all of them at the table, also unusual on a weekday. Dad's chair was empty, of course. And Mom didn't eat a thing.

"All set, Ty?" she said, meaning she was planning to drop him off at school and go to work, like normal. He got right up, maple syrup on his chin. Everyone was going to make normal things happen in the normal order. But at that moment the phone rang.

They all gazed at it. Grampy was the first to make a move, but Mom said, "I'll get it."

She answered the phone, listened for a moment, then covered the receiver with her hand. "Mr. Tulkinghorn," she said.

For a second or two Grampy seemed to shrink, actually grow smaller. Then he balled his hands into fists and straightened his spine, a great physical effort Ingrid could see on his face. "I'll take it in the other room, please, Carol," he said.

After he left, Ingrid said, "Is that about the plea deal?"

"I don't know," Mom said. "Here's some lunch money." She kissed Ingrid's forehead – not having to bend down much anymore – very quick, hardly touching. Ingrid caught a glimpse of Mom's eyes from close up; not good. "See you after school," Mom said.

Ingrid walked out of the kitchen but didn't head upstairs for her backpack. Instead she cut right, into the dining room. Grampy was on the phone, his back to her.

"Deadline?" he said.

Ingrid moved around the table, stood in front of him. He was listening so hard, she wasn't sure he saw her. Ingrid shook her head. Grampy noticed, covered the mouthpiece.

"What?" he said.

Ingrid just blurted it out. "Don't take the plea deal."

Grampy gazed down at her. "You don't understand," he said, his voice soft.

"Yes, I do," said Ingrid. "You're saving the farm, but it's not worth it."

Grampy's mood changed completely, and in an instant. He gave her that slit-eyed look – the one she'd hoped never to see again – and waved her away with the back of his hand.

Ingrid went to her room, found she was shaking. She started stuffing things into her backpack, hardly aware of what she was doing. Where was that stupid history packet, all about the War of 1812 or some other long-ago event that seemed meaningless right now? She opened the top desk drawer, rooted around. No sign of the packet, but here was the envelope with Grampy's parking garage stub. She took it out, gazed at it again. Then, as if to prove that nonbrain parts of the body could indeed sometimes take over the thinking department, her other hand reached in for her passbook from Central State Savings and Loan; reached in and took it out of the drawer. Her hands were telling her, *Get busy, Griddie. Fix what can be fixed. At least try.*

Ingrid opened the passbook. She had a balance of $316.72, mostly saved from babysitting and birthday money. The passbook and the parking stub went into the Velcro pocket in her backpack, almost by themselves, Ingrid more or less a spectator.

She took the bus to school. Getting off, she saw Mr. Samuels coming the other way, camera in hand.

"Hi, Mr. Samuels."

"Oh," he said, stopping short. "Ingrid." He looked a little embarrassed. Oh, no. Was it possible he'd heard this latest news already? Did that kind of personal stuff get printed in the paper? "I thought a picture of Mr. Sidney standing in front of the school bus would be nice."

"For the series?"

"That's right – he's next." Mr. Samuels moved toward the bus.

"What number is my grandfather going to be?"

Mr. Samuels turned. "Number?"

"In the series," Ingrid said. "When are you going to interview him?"

Again that embarrassed look, this time beyond doubt: so strange on Mr. Samuels's honest face, changing it from homely to ugly. "That's on hold now, I'm afraid," said Mr. Samuels.

"But he was a war hero. You said so yourself."

Mr. Samuels licked his lips; thin, colorless lips and a dry, colorless tongue. "Maybe after things get sorted out," he said.

Ingrid's voice rose, all by itself. "He didn't do it."

Mr. Samuels's eyes shifted to her, then away. "I'm sorry, Ingrid." He turned and knocked on the bus door.

Ingrid joined the line shuffling into Ferrand Middle. For some reason she was shuffling much slower than anyone else and soon found herself at the end of the line, and then even farther back, with space between her and the next kid. She came to a stop. Now her feet were doing the thinking. They turned her around, led her out of the parking lot, down the hill, and onto the street.

Ferrand Middle School stood on Park Road. Ingrid, who'd been trying to learn Echo Falls the way Holmes knew London, was sure that Park met High Street and that High met Spring and that Central State Savings and Loan was on Spring. She just wasn't clear on the very next step, right or left. She checked her compass ring.

Compass ring? *So you always know the directions:* Dad's words. Ingrid took off the compass ring and ground it under her heel. Then she turned left for no reason at all and started walking fast. Not long after, she came to Park. Yes. And not long after that – the wind behind her all the way – she was stepping up to the teller's counter at Central State Savings and Loan, withdrawal slip in hand.

She laid it on the counter.

"Why, Ingrid," said the teller, looking down. Oh, God, of course: Sylvia Breen, witch in *Hansel and Gretel* but in real life assistant head teller at Central State Savings and Loan. "No school today?"

"Um, well, the thing is," Ingrid began. "Research project!" She repeated it at normal volume. "Research project."

"That sounds exciting," said Mrs. Breen. She lowered her voice. "Can I tell you something in confidence?"

Ingrid nodded, getting ready for trouble.

"I'm having problems with my motivation."

Was it boring being a teller? Lots of people probably had boring jobs, and school wasn't so great either, but—

"I mean, for the life of me," said Mrs. Breen. "Why is she so set on pushing those two poor kids into the oven? She has plenty to eat – her whole house is made of candy."

"She is a witch, after all," Ingrid said.

"You think that's it?"

Ingrid nodded.

"Makes sense, I guess," said Mrs. Breen. "How would you like this?"

"This what?" said Ingrid.

Mrs. Breen tapped the withdrawal slip. "Your hundred dollars."

A lot of money, but New York was expensive; everyone knew that. "Twenties?" she said. But what if she needed something smaller? "Maybe a ten. And some fives." Would there be tipping? "And a few ones."

Mrs. Breen counted three twenties, a ten, five fives and five ones, snapping out the bills in an expert way. "Good luck on the project," she said.

Next: the train station. A potential problem, the train station being in the Flats, a run-down part of town pretty far from Central Savings and Loan. But Ingrid caught a break, the kind of break that said *Keep doing what you're doing*. There, parked on the other side of Spring Street, was a taxi. And the driver, chewing on a toothpick and reading a book: Murad, who'd driven her once before, and also ended up being one of the heroes of the Cracked-Up Katie case.

She crossed the street, tapped on his window. It slid down. "Ingrid, is it not?"

"Hi," said Ingrid. "The station, please."

"No schooling today?"

Ingrid tried that project thing again.

"Ah," said Murad. "American education – the standard of gold."

Ingrid got in the cab and off they went.

"I myself am experiencing American education at first hand," Murad said over his shoulder.

"You are?"

"Oh my yes. At the University of Hartford Extension."

Murad held up his book: *Principles of Accounting*. "Numbers, numbers, numbers – the fun I am having!"

"You like math?"

"Most certainly," said Murad. "Where else in this earthly life is everything clicking so beautifully into place?"

sixteen

"grand Central Terminal."

Despite everything, Ingrid felt some excitement when the conductor spoke those words, excitement to be all by herself in the Big Apple. She walked off the train with the other passengers, upstairs to the main concourse, huge and magnificent – the ceiling, all green and gold with stars, so high above. A realization struck Ingrid at that moment, unrelated to the mess her family was in or to Grampy's case: she would live in this city one day.

Someone bumped into her, almost knocking her down. Ingrid took her eyes off the ceiling. Everyone else's eyes were boring straight ahead, and they were all moving so fast. Lesson one on how to be a New Yorker. Ingrid spotted an elegant old lady carrying a tiny, pointy-faced dog and followed her onto the street.

Cold outside, with steam rising from vents here and there. The hard-edged shadow of a tall building angled down, dividing everything neatly into sun and shadow. The elegant old lady stepped into the sunny part, raised her hand, and called, "Taxi!"

A yellow taxi swerved over to the curb. The lady got in. She said, "Tiffany's, driver." The door closed and the taxi drove off, the dog gazing out the window looking snobby. Lesson two.

Ingrid stepped into the sunlight, raised her hand, and called, "Taxi!"

She barely got the word out before one screeched to a halt beside her. She was going to make a great old lady; although a dog like that was out of the question, no matter how elegant she ended up being.

"New York City Mercy Hospital, driver," she said, getting in.

Uh-oh. It was fun saying *driver* like that, as though she practically lived in taxis, but there was no sign that this driver had actually heard her. He was talking on a cell phone – wedged between shoulder and chin – in a foreign language, at the same time thumbing buttons on a handheld device. With the heel of his other hand he spun the wheel, sped into traffic so fast Ingrid felt g-forces, like an astronaut. He wheeled around a corner, then another, made a screaming stop followed by another lurching takeoff, honked several times, and almost hit a bike rider, two women with huge shopping bags, and a bus. Ingrid fumbled with her seat belt. It didn't work.

"Driver?" she said. "Sir?"

No answer. More sitting in traffic. More lurching. Then all at once a river appeared on the right, a wide river, sparkling in the sunshine. The East River? She almost asked the driver, but then he'd know what a rustic she was and maybe take advantage by driving miles and miles out of the way. That had happened to the Rubinos on Thanksgiving a couple of years before, when they'd gone past Yankee Stadium three times on their way to Radio City Music Hall. Instead, Ingrid checked the map on the back of the parking stub. It showed a highway running parallel to the river – FDR Drive. She looked around for a road sign, saw a little green one coming up, but before it was close enough to read, the taxi ducked into a tunnel. The driver raised his voice above the tunnel noise, suddenly said, "Okay, dude," before relapsing into the foreign language. Then they popped out of the tunnel, back into bright light, and another little green sign flashed by: FDR Drive. Yes!

A few minutes later the driver parked in front of a tall brick building on a quiet street. Over the door Ingrid read: NEW YORK CITY MERCY HOSPITAL, MAIN ENTRANCE. She paid, adding a one-dollar tip – anything less being pretty stingy, but anything more being reckless, especially seeing how she somehow had only $32.55 left – and got out.

The main entrance had a big revolving door, but not the kind you had to push: it moved as soon as it knew you were in there; nothing like that in Echo Falls. Ingrid went through and into the lobby. There were lots of people going back and forth, an information desk, and a bank of elevators at the back. Ingrid moved toward the information desk, but slowly. What was the next step? She didn't know; not that she hadn't tried to think it out that far, just that she hadn't come up with anything.

A man in a blue uniform sat behind the desk. She

approached him, toying with, *Hi, I need to know the exact times my grandfather was here* or *See this parking stub? Can you tell me if—*

The man at the desk turned to her. Ingrid had an instinctive reaction to his face: trouble. She swerved away, headed toward the back wall, pretended to examine the directory that hung there, listing the doctors. Then, all at once, her mind, so slow sometimes, so blind to the obvious, went back to Grampy's farm, the day he'd taught her how to chop wood. After, they'd gone inside for a hot drink. The phone had been ringing. Ingrid had answered. What then? A man calling for Grampy.

This is Doctor Pillman.

A funny name for a doctor, that was why she'd remembered. Then she'd handed the phone to Grampy. He'd listened and said, "Wrong number."

Ingrid scanned the directory, found six P's, listed not alphabetically but by floor, going up: Pradath, Pearl, Parsons, Phinney, Perez, Pillman. Dr. Eli Pillman, eleventh floor.

Ingrid moved toward the elevators, casting a sideways glance at the man in the blue uniform. He was talking to a woman with a cane.

Ding. An up arrow. Doors opened. Ingrid stepped into an empty elevator, pressed eleven, rode up. A sign above the buttons read: PLEASE RESPECT PATIENT CONFIDENTIALITY.

Ding. Ingrid stepped out. A woman in scrubs went by, reading from a blue folder; she didn't even look up. ELEVENTH FLOOR, read a sign on the wall: ONCOLOGY. Ingrid didn't know what that meant. An arrow pointed left for the ward, OR, and radiology, right for doctors' offices. Ingrid went right, down a long corridor. Dr. Pillman's office was at the end. The door opened as Ingrid reached for the knob.

An orderly came out, pushing a little old bald person in a wheelchair. On second look, not a little old person but a kid – a girl – of about her own age. She wore one of those double *x* Rollexxes on her wrist, red like Ingrid's, and had a blue folder in her lap. The girl's eyes met Ingrid's. Ingrid tried to say hi but her throat closed up. The orderly pushed the wheelchair down the hall. Ingrid went into Dr. Pillman's office.

She was in a waiting room, not unlike the waiting room of Dr. Binkerman, her orthodontist in Echo Falls. In fact the blond-wood furniture looked identical, and so did the paintings on the wall – all of them about Venice: palaces, canals, gondolas. No one was waiting in Dr. Pillman's waiting room. Behind the window of the reception area at the back, a woman with her hair in a bun and glasses halfway down her nose sat at a computer, her profile toward Ingrid. The walls of her room were lined with shelves of blue folders.

Ingrid sat in one of the blond-wood chairs. She picked up a *National Geographic* with a volcano on the cover. A phone rang softly behind the glass. The woman answered. Ingrid couldn't hear what she was saying, just saw how she shook her head no, a decisive head shake that meant no for sure.

Ingrid gazed at a page of *National Geographic*, unseeing. She tried and tried to think of what to say to the woman behind the glass partition. Nothing she came up with – whether she started right off the top with the murder of Harris Thatcher or left it out completely, led to any response from the woman other than "Does your grandfather know you're here?"

And then what? A call to Grampy? A call home to Mom? Downward spiral, essence of.

She heard a little squeak and glanced up. The receptionist's window slid open a foot or two and the woman looked out at her. Uh-oh.

"You must be Libby's sister," the woman said. "I've heard so much about you."

"Uh," said Ingrid.

"She should be back soon," the woman said. "These tests don't take long."

Ingrid nodded, stared down at her *National Geographic*, open, she now saw, at a bright color photograph of a Latin American bride trying on her wedding gown. Then the side door of the reception room opened and the woman came out, walking quickly. She stopped right in front of Ingrid; a tall woman with sharp features. Ingrid got ready to make a full confession.

"I'm going to grab a quick sandwich," the woman said. "Get you anything?"

"No, thanks," said Ingrid.

The woman gazed down at her for a moment. "You do look alike," she said. Then she turned and left the office, closing the door behind her.

A quick sandwich: How quick? From where? And Libby, the girl in the wheelchair, would be back soon, back from some test. Ingrid felt sleazy, a brand-new feeling that disgusted her. She wanted to jump up, run out the door, get far, far away. But: Grampy was about to cut a deal for something he didn't do, and the proof might be in one of those blue folders she could see through the receptionist's window. *Fix what can be fixed. At least try.*

The next thing Ingrid knew, she was on her feet. The air seemed to be buzzing, like a scary soundtrack. This was a time for speed, but for some reason she couldn't have been slower – crossing the waiting room, opening the receptionist's door, going inside, all of that like a sleepwalker.

There were hundreds of blue folders, maybe thousands. The shelves lined the entire back wall, floor to ceiling, and parts of both side walls. How would she ever—

Whoa. What were those? Letter stickers here and there on the edges of the shelves, *A* to *Z*. *H* was along the back wall, second shelf from the bottom. Ingrid grabbed a file, read the name tag: Heller. She pawed through. Henley, Hersheiser, Hester, Hibbs, Hill. She pulled it out. Alice.

But the next one was Hill, Aylmer. She opened the folder. Grampy's file was thinner than most of them, just five or six pages inside. Ingrid scanned them; now, when slowing down was important, she was going much too fast, didn't understand a thing. She forced herself to put on the brakes, go back, even mouth some of the words. There were lots she didn't understand – like unresectable, metastasis, palliative – but lots she did. Like dates, for example. Dr. Pillman had signed a form admitting Grampy to New York City Mercy Hospital at 11:57

a.m. on Tuesday, February 11, three minutes before the beginning of the three-hour period when Mr. Thatcher was murdered. He'd spent four nights on the eleventh-floor ward – there were notes in the chart for every one, signed by various doctors and nurses – and then Dr. Pillman had discharged him at 9:30 a.m., Saturday, February 15. Grampy was innocent and could prove it, even prove it easily. That was a fact, beyond all possible doubt.

Also beyond all possible doubt: he had cancer – and not just cancer, but inoperable cancer. Ingrid formed and re-formed that word *inoperable* in her mind, hoping she could make it mean something else.

And one more thing: bottom of the last page – it was shaking in her hand – a note signed *Eli Pillman, MD*: *The patient has repeatedly and adamantly forbidden any and all contact by Mercy staff with his family, friends, or associates. An offer to confer with a Mercy psychologist or clergyperson was refused in unqualified terms. Patient also referred to the certainty of legal action if his wishes were not "obeyed to the letter".*

Ingrid closed the folder, slid it back into place on the shelf next to Hill, Alice. The buzzing had grown louder in her ears, was becoming unbearable. She hurried from the receptionist's office, crossed the waiting room, slung on her backpack, her movements all jerky now. Then: out the door, down the hall to the elevators, trying not to run.

Ding. Going down. Ingrid got in the elevator. The doors started to close. Across the hall the doors of another elevator opened. Dr. Pillman's receptionist stepped out, coffee cup in hand. She saw Ingrid. The expression on her face began to change.

seventeen

data. Now she had lots, but what good did it do?

Ingrid sat beside a window on the northbound train, an empty seat between her and the nearest passenger, a man typing nonstop on his laptop. The sun, popping up from time to time over trees or between buildings, was slowly sinking in the sky, growing fatter and more orange. She checked the time on her red Rollexx, a watch she'd always see differently now: 3:35. The kids would be on the buses, or already home.

Data. One: Grampy was innocent. Two: He had cancer. Three: He didn't want anyone to know.

But Ingrid, no respecter of patient confidentiality, did know. So now what? Tell Chief Strade? How could she? That would be betraying Grampy. And in a crazy way she could never explain, betraying Grampy somehow got all mixed up with not respecting Libby, betraying her, too. She'd ended up spying on both of them. Ingrid shivered. The man with the laptop glanced over. She stared straight ahead.

Crime is common, Holmes told Watson in "The Adventure of the Copper Beeches". *Logic is rare.* Ingrid had puzzled over that more than once, still wasn't sure what Holmes was driving at. Watson hadn't been sure either, as she recalled, getting kind of fed up with Holmes in that scene. How could logic help her now?

Grampy was innocent. He had an alibi he wouldn't use. She couldn't betray his wish, and at the same time also couldn't allow him to go to jail. But someone should go to jail, all right, because Mr. Thatcher was dead, the most important fact of—

Whoa. Ingrid sat up straight. Mr. Thatcher was dead. Someone – not Grampy – had killed him. Therefore, finding out the identity of that someone let Grampy off the hook without revealing his secret. Logic, pure and simple, maybe the rarest type. *But so slow in coming, Griddie.* Why? Was it because she'd been spending all her mental energy on the alibi, worried deep down that it didn't exist, leaving open the possibility of Grampy's guilt? Ingrid didn't know; it no longer mattered, any-way. Her task was clear, a task to be done on her own, of course, since the law had already made up its mind. On her own and fast: with that plea deal deadline, time was running out. Ingrid glanced out the window, saw countryside she recognized. She picked her backpack off the floor and slung it on, not wanting to lose a second.

"Echo Falls," said the conductor.

Ingrid got off the train alone, walked across the tracks and through the station – so tiny, almost like a toy building after Grand Central – and onto the street. No one around. Getting dark now down in the Flats, maybe four or five miles from home, but Ingrid was pretty sure she knew the way. You went left, followed Station Street to Factory Road, took Factory Road up that steep hill with Le Zinc at the top, a dark little restaurant but Mom's favorite in Echo Falls, in fact where she and Dad always went on their anni—

All at once, Ingrid was crying, there on the station steps, a big round lamp over her head. What was wrong with her? This was no good. For one thing, she had no time, and for another, it turned out that there was someone around after all, because headlights flashed on across the street. And the car? Oh, no. An Echo Falls police cruiser, the one with CHIEF on the side. Ingrid froze. The cruiser made a quick U-turn and stopped right beside her. Chief Strade looked out his window.

"Ingrid?" he said.

She wiped her face on her sleeve, very quick.

He got out of the car, stared down at her; so big. "You all right?" he said; and that voice, soft on top, deep and rumbly underneath.

She nodded.

"By yourself?" he said.

She nodded again.

"Just hanging around the station?" he said.

Ingrid opened her mouth to say yes, a pretty ridiculous answer, but before she could get the word out, he had a follow-up question.

"Or coming from somewhere?" he said.

A tricky one. She gazed up at him, trying to read

something in his eyes. All she saw was that overhead light, reflected twice.

"Happened to be talking to Murad today," the chief said. "You know Murad, drives for Town Taxi?"

"Murad? Uh, I—"

"A good man, Murad," said the chief. "A good citizen. We often touch base, Murad and I."

Murad was some kind of police informer? "Oh," said Ingrid.

"Good citizen," the chief said again, as though making a point with just those two words. "Naturally, he was concerned – this being a school day."

Murad's talk about projects, American education, gold standard – was that all fake? Was everybody – like Dad – just faking it, twenty-four seven? Could you take anything at face value?

"Concerned about you, Ingrid," said the chief. "And so am I."

"I'm fine," Ingrid said.

The chief shifted slightly. Now she could see his eyes. The message in them was *You don't look fine.* "How about hopping in the car? I'll drive you home."

"That's all right," said Ingrid.

"You're headed someplace else?"

"No."

"Then hop in. It's no trouble."

No way out of it, at least no way that came to her. She got in, sitting up front beside Chief Strade. He pulled away from the station. Just a few weeks ago Ingrid would have felt very safe driving along with the chief like this. And now? The opposite. How could it be otherwise? He was trying to put Grampy away.

"Got a leftover candy cane or two in the glove compartment," the chief said.

"No, thanks."

"With the red stripes."

Ingrid shook her head.

They drove in silence, along Station and up Factory Road, just as Ingrid had thought. Lights shone on the windows of Le Zinc, and there were lots of cars in the parking lot, one a silver TT like … like Dad's. Yes, almost certainly Dad's, although Ingrid couldn't read the plate – and what was this? Parked right beside the TT: a green hatchback. Chief Strade turned a corner and Le Zinc dropped out of sight. Ingrid felt dizzy, maybe like she was about to be sick.

"Feeling okay?" said the chief.

"Fine," said Ingrid.

Her window slid down an inch or two. She breathed in the cold fresh air, breathed it in deeply, felt a little better.

The chief cleared his throat. "What would you have done in my place?" he said.

"About what?" said Ingrid, figuring he was going to start in on some justification for railroading Grampy.

"About hearing that a thirteen-year-old kid you knew was down by the train station by herself on a school day," he said.

I would have minded my own damn business. But Ingrid kept that answer to herself. "Nothing," she said.

"You would have done nothing?" he said. "When your job is to protect the people of the town?"

"You told my par— my mom."

"Should have," said the chief. "But I didn't. You— There's enough trouble right now."

Whose fault was that? Ingrid found herself glaring at the chief. His eyes shifted away. Hard to explain, but at that moment she was pretty sure that Dad had used his alibi, or enough of it that the chief had guessed the rest.

"What I did do," he said, "was ask the station clerk where you went."

"And he told you?"

"Grand Central Terminal, return ticket."

Anger came boiling up out of her. She'd never felt like this. "I'll sue him."

The chief's head turned toward her. Then he laughed. Had she ever heard him laugh before? A low, musical kind of laugh. It made her even madder.

"Sorry, Ingrid. I'm not laughing at you."

"No?"

"No. There's just something about how you—" He stopped himself. "Sure you don't want one of those candy canes?"

"I already told you."

Any amusement drained from his voice, fast. "Bet you can guess my next question."

Ingrid knew the next question, all right, but she said, "I have no idea." That sounded a lot like Chloe Ferrand, her friend-slash-enemy, Echo Falls rich girl; some of that anger got diverted toward herself.

"The next question," said the chief. "What were you doing in New York?"

That was the question she couldn't answer, not

without betraying Grampy. But at that moment Ingrid found herself in the grip of a powerful desire to tell Chief Strade everything: New York City Mercy Hospital, Grampy's cancer, Libby, and yes, Dad and Mrs. McGreevy too. Maybe even Dad and Mrs. McGreevy first, and how selfish did that make her? Ingrid bit the inside of her cheeks – so hard she tasted blood – and remained silent.

"I could look into it, you know," the chief said.

Ingrid nodded. Good luck to him: the tracks were doubly covered, hers and Grampy's.

"The way you nod like that," said the chief, "kind of tells me I wouldn't have a prayer."

Ingrid didn't answer.

They turned off High Street, into Riverbend. "Hope you know what you're doing, Ingrid," the chief said.

He didn't speak the rest of the way. Or almost. On the way down Avondale, where the town woods first came into view, all dark now under a clear evening sky, they passed a car parked by an empty lot. The chief slowed down. Ingrid saw that the parked car had a mudded-out plate.

"What the hell?" said the chief. He pulled over beside the parked car, shone his flashlight inside, then drove on. "One thing I don't like seeing around here," he said. "Private operators."

"What's that?" said Ingrid.

"Private detectives," the chief said. "Private eyes. They muddy everything up."

"Just like the license plate."

"Exactly," he said. He gave her a long look. "Exactly.

I know this car – belongs to a dirt-ball PI from Bridgeport, name of Meinhof. Dieter Meinhof."

Dieter Meinhof. Dirt-ball PI from Bridgeport who'd snapped her picture, and also the anonymous tipster: any reason not to tell the chief about that? Ingrid hadn't made up her mind when he turned onto Maple Lane, stopped in front of 99: lights on in the house, no cars in the driveway. The chief checked his rearview mirror. He wanted to get going – she could feel it.

"Take care of yourself," the chief said.

"Thanks for the ride," said Ingrid.

She went in through the garage; no car there either. And no one in the kitchen. "Hey! Anyone home?"

No response.

She opened the door to the basement, didn't hear the TV or any weights clanking around, called out anyway: "Ty?"

No response.

Ingrid checked the hall, dining room, went into the living room. A fire burned low in the fireplace. Fresh logs filled the wood box. And Grampy lay sleeping on the couch, still wearing his boots and the red-and-black-checked lumber jacket. She watched him, his chest rising and falling, slow and regular. Did he look sick? Not to her. Just tired, maybe. Her mind flashed a picture of Mr. Thatcher lying in the snow, also wearing a red-and-black-checked lumber jacket, but chest still and skin blue. Grampy was a long way from that. His chest went up and down, up and down. Was there any law against hope?

She heard the side door open, went into the kitchen. Ty was taking off his jacket, his varsity football jacket with *Red Raiders* on the back, his number *19* on one sleeve and *Ty* on the other.

"Where've you been?" he said. "Mom's pissed."

"Oh, God – is she out looking for me?"

"Had to go in to the office," Ty said. "I told her you were at the Rubinos'."

"Thanks. Did she say anything about Dad?"

Ty opened the fridge, drank OJ from the carton, put it back without replacing the cap. Chaos was on the way.

"She's going to talk to us tomorrow after school," he said. "They both are."

"Dad and her together?"

"Guess so."

"That means they must have been talking."

"Guess so," said Ty again.

"What are they going to say?"

"That everything's back to normal."

"You think so?"

"Get real," Ty said. He picked his backpack off the butcher block, started toward the door.

Ingrid glanced over at the water bowl. "Where's Nigel?"

"Stupid dog," said Ty, waving his hand in the direction of the woods.

"What do you mean?"

"I took him for a walk to the tree house and he ran away," Ty said.

"Ran away? We've got to find him."

"Where do you think I've been for the last half hour?"

"You just gave up?"

"He'll come back as soon as he realizes there's no food out there." Ty left the room, clomped upstairs.

"But he's never run away before," Ingrid said to nobody. She ran down to the basement, threw open one of the sliding doors. "Nigel!" she called at the top of her lungs. "Nigel!"

She listened.

No response.

Chaos, closing in fast. Ingrid hunted around for a flashlight, her movements jerky, panic awakening inside.

eighteen

ingrid stepped into the night, closing the slider and switching on a flashlight, the long rubberized one from the furnace room. She shone the light around the backyard, saw a whole muddle of footprints.

Overhead the sky was clear and full of stars. An odd thought hit her at that moment, maybe an obvious one: The stars were up there in the daytime too; it was just that you could only see them at night. She felt a funny pressure in her head, a feeling she'd had before, always followed by a little spark of inspiration going off. *Bzzz*. But no *bzzz* this time: the feeling just faded away, leaving that promising thought – stars in the daytime – just hanging there.

Ingrid crossed the yard, started up the path through the woods. She angled the beam downward: Now there were only three sets of tracks, two outgoing, one incoming. One set of outgoing prints matched the incoming – flat prints with horizontal grooves at the front and back. Those would be Ty's sneakers; like all

178

Echo Falls boys, he didn't bother with boots in the winter. Like all Echo Falls boys except Joey, she realized. She could picture Joey's boots, all scuffed up, strapped into his snowshoes when they'd walked the old Indian trail. *Indian trail* – the name made a connection in her mind with that stubborn cowlick of his, the blunt Indian feather thing. There was something different about Joey. She missed him.

The other set of prints, of course, was Nigel's. At first he'd kept to the straight and narrow, his paws – the front left one bigger than the other three for some reason – running parallel to the sneaker tracks, meaning he'd been on the leash. Not long after the turnoff to the huge oak with the double trunk – Ingrid could see it, a thick shadow between thinner ones – where Dad had built the tree house years before, Nigel's prints veered suddenly toward the right. Off the leash. But Ty's kept going straight ahead, spaced the same, meaning he wasn't running, didn't feel he'd lost control of Nigel. Sure enough, ten or twenty feet farther on, Nigel's prints came angling out of the woods, back beside Ty's.

A little way beyond that, Nigel veered off again. Ty's tracks continued normally for ten or twelve steps, then began to lengthen, meaning he'd walked faster or even run. After a while these faster tracks came to an end, doubled back, went forward, doubled back again. Ingrid could picture Ty pacing back and forth, yelling, "Nigel! Nigel!"

She tried it too, cupping her hands to her mouth. "Nigel! Nigel!"

No response. The woods were silent. Ingrid looked

up through the bare branches: all those stars. The universe was infinite, meaning it went on forever, Dad said. Therefore we were tinier than tiny, just about not there at all. In *Casablanca* – the reason Ingrid was Ingrid – the café owner, Humphrey Bogart, says something about the problems of a few little people not amounting to a hill of beans in this world. Maybe not; but then what was the point of the movie? Ingrid turned back, shining the light with care, and picked up Nigel's tracks where he'd left the path.

Off the path lay unpacked snow, harder going, but Nigel's tracks were very clear. He'd cut between two big trees, then circled a prickly bush, its branches sagging with snow, the distance between his paw prints short and unvarying, in no particular hurry. Up a long, gradual rise, the trees growing thicker, Nigel kept to that deliberate pace, straight ahead, like he had a plan, was actually going somewhere.

"Nigel! Nigel!"

Silence.

Just past a fallen tree – a fallen tree that Nigel had walked around but that Ingrid stepped over – she came to a small clearing. She swept the beam ahead, following Nigel's tracks. They led to the middle of the clearing, spreading out, like he had started running, and then – what was this? They seemed to vanish, as though Nigel had suddenly taken flight. Ingrid went closer, saw that where Nigel's prints ended, the snow was all messed up, full of holes and ridges, as though there'd been lots of activity. No way that he'd simply vanished; therefore maybe his prints continued beyond the messed-up patch, on the other side. Ingrid raised the light, but at that moment it flickered twice and went out.

Night closed in right away. Ingrid couldn't see a thing. She tapped at the lens, turned the switch off and on, shook the flashlight, thumped it against her leg. Nothing.

Her eyes began to adjust to the darkness, but only to a point. The whiteness of the snow in the clearing was now a faint glow; Nigel's footprints and the messed-up patch remained invisible. All around rose the trees, their tops dark and spiky against the starry sky. She banged the flashlight against her leg again, harder this time. The top fell off with a *spronging* sound and the batteries shot out, landing with soft thuds. Ingrid got on her knees, felt with her mittened hands in the snow. She was still doing that, without success, when a dog barked, far far away, almost inaudible.

"Nigel? Nigel?"

She listened.

"Nigel? Nigel?"

The dog did not bark again.

Ingrid rose. No light. What else could she do but go home? She went back across the clearing, left its dull glow for the complete darkness of the woods. Or almost complete darkness: there were still those stars above. Sailors long ago, like Columbus and Magellan, knew how to read them, could navigate by the stars. Ingrid didn't know how to read the stars, but she was close to home, so – no problem. All she had to do was follow the slope downhill until she reached the path, very simple navigation. Even if she couldn't see the path, she'd feel the space around her opening up, and then all she'd have to do was turn left and soon her own backyard would—

Ow. Ingrid bumped into something hard, right across her shins. The fallen tree? She reached down, felt tough bark, all nubbly. Yes, the fallen tree – meaning her sense of direction wasn't letting her down. Columbus, Magellan, and Griddie: Three Navigatin' Dudes, as Brucie would probably say. Oh, God: was Brucie starting to rub off on her? Ingrid climbed over the fallen tree and kept going.

Thinking of Brucie reminded her of the play. Like Gretel, she was now in the dark forest. Unlike Gretel – hey, *Gretel*, not so different from *Griddie* – she wasn't afraid; she'd played in these woods for years. And very soon she did feel space opening up around her, saw the faint glow of the path. Left turn. Ninety-nine Maple Lane was seven or eight minutes away, tops. Might help to know exactly how long the walk took. Data, right? Ingrid checked her red Rollexx, pressing the light button. Seven fifty-two. Should be home by eight.

She walked on, sensed the turnoff to the tree house on her right. Twinkling lights from 99 Maple Lane and maybe some of the neighboring houses would be coming into view any second. But they didn't; probably blocked by the trees. Ingrid picked up the pace, not so easy, the snow on the path somehow less packed down than before. She was sinking to her ankles with practically every step, also huffing and puffing a little. She checked the time again: 8:09? That didn't seem right.

Ingrid paused, glanced around, saw nothing but dark shapes. Was this going to end in embarrassment, with her screaming "Help! Help!" in the night? In her haste she'd forgotten hat and mittens; now she felt how cold it was. Embarrassment or worse. Fear awoke inside her. The first thing it did was try to make her breathless.

"Get a grip," she said aloud, and then remembered that time in the kitchen with Mom, trying to find the right voice for Gretel, and the question that had risen in her mind: *Did real bravery start like that, just making a bit of an effort to control fear?* Ingrid kept going, making a bit of an effort to control fear. And not long after – at 8:16, to be exact – twinkling lights appeared between the trees. Strange how her estimates had been so far off. She'd walked this path so often, at least the first part from the backyard to the Punch Bowl, that you'd think by now she'd—

Streetlights appeared, but not the streetlights of Maple Lane. Ingrid walked out of the woods and into a vacant lot. Vacant lot? Was this Avondale? Yes. Ingrid glanced back, saw she'd followed some completely different path. No problem in the end: home was right around the corner. She crossed the vacant lot, stepped onto the street – at the same spot, it suddenly occurred to her, where Chief Strade had pulled over to examine the car with the mudded-out plates. The car with the mudded-out plates was no longer around.

Ingrid walked toward the corner. She heard someone driving up behind her. No sidewalks in Riverbend: she moved to the edge of the road. Headlights shone on her; Ingrid's shadow grew long. Then the car slowed down. Ingrid turned: not a sedan with mudded-out plates, but the MPV.

It stopped beside her. Mom leaned across the front seat, called through the open passenger window, "Ingrid? What are you doing out at this hour?"

"Nigel ran away."

"For God's sake. How can you be so careless? Get in."

Ingrid got in.

"Don't sit on the listing sheets."

"Sorry." Ingrid moved the listing sheets aside. Mom drove home. As they turned into the driveway – no sign of Nigel waiting on the front lawn – Ingrid said, "Do you think he'll come back, Mom?"

"I wouldn't let him," Mom said. Her voice broke and then she was sobbing.

"Mom! Don't cry. I meant Nigel."

Mom didn't seem to hear. She slumped forward on the steering wheel, crying and crying. "Don't be a fool like me, Ingrid," she said. "Whatever you do."

"You're not a fool, Mom." Ingrid patted Mom's back. It felt bony, even under her coat.

Mom pulled herself together, got a tissue from her purse, dabbed at her face. "Sorry, Ingrid. That won't happen again." She smiled a little smile, not real, but at least her face took the shape of a smile, if only for a moment. *Just making a bit of an effort to control fear.* Mom was brave, no question. "I'm sure Nigel will be back soon," she said. "He probably followed some scent." After a pause, Mom added, "He'll get tired of that soon enough."

"Yeah," said Ingrid, crossing her fingers.

nineteen

ingrid awoke just before dawn, a milky half-light faint in the space between her curtains. She felt tired, as though she'd been up all night, although Ingrid actually didn't know that feeling – she and Stacy had tried twice to stay up all night, both efforts ending in zonked-out failure somewhere between four and five a.m. But her first thought was: Nigel. She got right up – the floor so cold under her bare feet – threw on clothes, went downstairs. Had Nigel come home in the night, scratched at the door or barked, and been let in by Mom?

No Nigel: not lying by the water bowl, the front door, on the old corduroy couch in the TV room – not in any of his usual places. She turned from the couch, looked out the sliders, where Nigel liked to appear when he knew TV watching was going on without him; he was partial to the cooking shows. No Nigel: but what was this? Snow. Snow and lots of it, falling fast, the flakes big and dense. Oh, no.

Ingrid put on jacket, mittens, hat, strapped on her snowshoes, went outside. A snowflake landed on her eyelash, so fat and heavy she actually felt its weight. Not a print to be seen: the snow lay smooth and unmarked, across the backyard and onto the trail. All the tracks, all the evidence from the night before, Nigel's, Ty's, and her own – wiped out. She hurried down the trail, past the turnoff to the tree house, searching for the spot where Nigel had veered off the trail for good. If only she hadn't got lost on the way back last night – that idea, timing the walk, would have worked.

Ingrid kept going. The snow wasn't coming down so hard in the woods; it was more like being inside a snow globe after someone has given it a good shake. How much farther? She remembered that right after Nigel had left the path, he'd gone between two trees and then around a spiky bush. She looked for a triangle like that and saw hundreds, every sharp detail and hard edge blurred by snowflakes and milky light.

Thump. Snow fell from a branch high above and landed a few feet away. Ingrid took that as a sign and left the path.

She went between two trees, two more, then past a bush, not very spiky, and a rock, not as big as the one near the Punch Bowl with RED RAIDERS RULE spray-painted on the side, but pretty big. Could she have missed a rock like that in the night? Ingrid didn't know. She glanced around, saw nothing that might help her.

"Nigel! Nigel!"

No response. But her voice hardly carried, muffled by the snow. She tried again, louder. Nothing.

Ingrid moved on. The ground began sloping up. For some reason her legs didn't have their normal strength. She leaned forward and pushed, head down. She almost missed the fallen tree, about twenty feet to her right, now half buried in snow. A minute or two later she stepped into the clearing.

Those clues from last night – Nigel's tracks and the messed-up patch where it looked like some commotion had happened: all gone, the surface smooth and unfeatured. Ingrid walked to the middle of the clearing, trying to picture what had happened. Nigel had left the path and set off through the woods on a straight line to this place, picking up speed. Then his tracks ended in the messed-up patch. And therefore? No idea. She paced around, tired and frustrated. The metal-toothed piece under her right snowshoe – crampon? – suddenly dug into something hard; maybe not hard, but denser than the snow.

Ingrid crouched down, swept snow aside and uncovered … a steak? Yes, a T-bone steak, a cooked one with grill marks and spices sprinkled on top; and one ragged bite taken out of the side, not the polite kind of bite cut with knife and fork. Ingrid picked up the T-bone steak, sniffed at it, and then noticed something strange: a tangled thread – no, not a thread, more like fishing line, one end knotted around the joining part of that T in the T-bone. She untangled it: surprisingly long, ten or twelve feet.

And the meaning? A picture began taking shape in her mind. She turned in the direction Nigel had come from, in that beeline, and as she did, the frame of her left snowshoe clinked on something metallic. Ingrid looked down, saw a disk. She picked it up: one of those tags from the vet that attaches to a dog collar, proving the dog has had its shots. *Riverbend Veterinary Medicine,* she read. Then came the vet's phone number, and at the bottom the name of the dog: *Nigel.*

She pocketed Nigel's tag. Then she laid the T-bone in the snow, moved across the clearing with the end of the line in her hand till it was straight. She tugged on the line. The steak slid across the snow.

The picture grew sharper in her mind, a picture with two characters. One was a T-bone–loving dog with a great sense of smell. The other character was a creepy-looking fat-faced guy with a T-bone steak on a fishing line ... and what else? A cage? Maybe. This second character lured the T-bone lover into the clearing, the T-bone lover probably out of control by now, with the proof that his sense of smell was world-class practically in his grasp. All character two had to do was drag that steak right up to the open cage door. But the next step, the actual capture, hadn't gone smoothly. The messed-up patch and the tag coming loose off the collar proved that. There'd been a struggle, a struggle that Nigel had lost. Otherwise his prints would have continued somewhere beyond the patch, and last night she'd seen none.

And then? The creepy guy had carried the cage out of the woods, taking the path that Ingrid had found by accident – the path that ended at Avondale Road. He had a car parked there, a car with mudded-out plates – Dieter Meinhof, *dirt-ball PI from Bridgeport.* Ingrid knew what had happened, knew who had done it, when, and how. But why? Was there some connection between Nigel and Bridgeport? Nigel and the anonymous caller? She had no clue.

Snow fell harder and the wind rose, driving the flakes, smaller and icier now, across the clearing, but Ingrid was barely aware. *PI* meant *private investigator*. There were public investigators too – Chief Strade for example, maybe a good one in general but he'd botched the Thatcher case, arresting an innocent man. But that wasn't the point, not right now. The point was that Chief Strade worked for the public, meaning the people of Echo Falls. And a private eye? He worked for somebody private, a client. And now it came, one of those buzzes of inspiration. *Bzzz.* Dieter Meinhof didn't kidnap Nigel for himself but for a client, someone who paid him to do it. Someone had also paid him to make the anonymous call. Could it have been the same person?

And if so, who?

"Nigel!" she called. "Nigel?" But there was no way she could outshout this storm, and Ingrid didn't really try.

Back home, Ingrid went upstairs. Mom was talking on the phone behind her closed bedroom door. Ingrid raised her hand to knock, all set to tell Mom about Nigel. Then she heard Mom say, "Let's just get it over with." Ingrid could tell Mom was trying not to cry. She backed away, went into her own room, got ready for school.

Mom was in the kitchen when Ingrid came down, just staring out the window, a cup of coffee in her hand.

"Ingrid?"

"Yeah?"

"What are you doing up? It's a snow day. That's why I didn't wake you."

"Oh," said Ingrid; first snow day in her life when she hadn't jumped up and down at the news.

"You can go back to bed if you want," Mom said. "But when the snow stops, we're going out to the farm."

"What for?"

"We have to talk, all of us."

"Dad too?"

"Yes," Mom said. "Him too. You and Ty have to understand that your lives will still be" – Mom searched for a word – "stable."

"I do," Ingrid said, although she felt far from stable.

"You have to hear it from both of us," Mom said.

Ingrid went over, gave Mom a hug. No tears this time, just a quiet hug, snow coming down like crazy outside. Ingrid had a momentary feeling of being all grown up. It vanished the moment she let go.

"Hi," Dad said, opening the door to the farmhouse.

They went in, Ingrid, Mom, Ty, all of them keeping their distance from Dad. He wore a leather jacket Ingrid had never seen before, looked good except for a shaving cut under his lower lip.

"Fresh coffee," he said. "And there's hot chocolate for the kids." They sat at the kitchen table and Dad set mugs in front of everyone. Hot chocolate just the way Ingrid liked it, with a marshmallow floating at the top: a bit surprising that Dad knew that. She didn't even touch the mug. Mom sat back, arms folded. Ty's eyes were on Dad, the lids partly closed in a way that reminded Ingrid of those shooting slits in the wall of a fort.

"Ty," Dad said. "Ingrid. I know you're angry at me. You have every right. There are just two things I want you to know. The first is your lives are going to change as little as possible. You'll still be living in the same house with Mom, going to the same schools, doing everything the same."

"We get it," Ty said. "The same."

Dad flinched slightly, as though dodging a blow.

"Ty," said Mom.

"And what's the second thing?" said Ingrid.

Dad looked right at her. "The second thing is I love you both very much."

"You got them in the wrong order," Ty said.

The very best thing Ty had said in his whole life. Ingrid felt herself flushing, filled with pride, as though for some great champion knight of the Middle Ages.

Dad went pale. That lump of muscle in his jaw bulged. "Come on, Ty," he said. "We—"

"We?" said Ty. He rose and walked to the door without another word. Mom sat with her arms folded. Dad's mouth opened but no words came out. Ingrid rose too, without a thought, and followed Ty outside.

The wind lifted his unzipped jacket, like wings. Ty looked so big. At first he didn't notice her.

"Hey," Ingrid said.

He turned to her. Big, maybe, but his face was miserable. "Hey," he said, very quiet.

"You da man," said Ingrid.

A pause. Then Ty laughed, and didn't look so miserable anymore.

"Let's go see the pig," Ingrid said.

They went into the barn. Piggy was in his pen, as expected. The surprise was the man standing beside it, stripping the wrapper off a Slim Jim. The man heard them coming in and turned.

"Mr. Sidney?"

"Hi, petunia," Mr. Sidney said, and to Ty, "Hi, kid." He wore his Battle of the Coral Sea cap, also had a cigar in his mouth. Mr. Sidney smoked? Ingrid realized she'd never seen him except on the school bus.

"What are you—" she began, and then it hit her. "You're the one taking care of the pig for Grampy?"

"Course," said Mr. Sidney.

Piggy, tiny eyes on that Slim Jim, made a strange sound between grunt and squeal, an impatient sound.

"You and Grampy are friends?" Ingrid said.

"Wouldn't go that far," said Mr. Sidney. "Not so easy being friends with Aylmer Hill, no offense. But there's nothing I wouldn't do for him."

"Huh?" said Ty.

"Wasn't for your grandfather, there'd be no Myron Emmitt Sidney standing before your eyes this very moment," said Mr. Sidney. "Would've been long gone, dead and buried in a far-off grave, ancient history."

He let go of the Slim Jim. Piggy scarfed it down in midair.

"Are you talking about the war, Mr. Sidney?" Ingrid said.

Mr. Sidney tipped his cap.

twenty

"**know** much about the war in the Pacific?" said Mr. Sidney. They sat by the pigpen on rickety old stools left over from back when Grampy had kept some cows. "World War Two, I'm talking about."

"Pearl Harbor," Ty said.

"Yup," said Mr. Sidney. He puffed on his cigar. The mouth end was all raggedy and the smoke smelled horrible. "Anything else?"

"You and Grampy fought on Corregidor," Ingrid said. "And Major Ferrand."

"Yup," said Mr. Sidney. "They teach you where Corregidor is?"

"Who?" said Ingrid.

"Your teachers. Who else?"

"An island?" Ingrid said.

"An island in Manila Bay, south of the Bataan Peninsula," Mr. Sidney said. "Philippines, I'm talking about." He licked his finger – knuckles swollen and deformed – leaned down, and drew a map in the dust on the worn wide-plank floor. "Corregidor," he said. "Manila. Bataan. Got it so far?"

Ingrid and Ty nodded.

"Don't need to tell you where the Philippines are, do I?" said Mr. Sidney.

Ingrid and Ty shook their heads.

Maybe not convincingly, because Mr. Sidney added, "Western Pacific – leave it at that." He tapped a big white ash off his cigar, ground it under his heel. "Thing to remember is" – he took another puff – "we got cut off."

"Cut off?" said Ty.

"On account of it being an island chain, the Philippines, and their fleet still ruling the waves, the whole point of Pearl Harbor. Midway came later."

They looked at him blankly.

"Midway being the beginning of our comeback, fleet-wise," said Mr. Sidney. "But forget all that. Just remember…" His voice trailed off and his eyes went a little vague.

"That we got cut off?" Ingrid said.

"Right," said Mr. Sidney. "April, nineteen hundred and forty-two."

"That's when Corregidor fell?" said Ingrid.

"Nope – that's when Bataan fell. Fall of Corregidor wasn't till May. Lot of people don't realize that, but it makes big difference."

"Why?" said Ty.

"Because the boys caught up in Bataan went on the march, and the boys down in Corregidor did not," Mr. Sidney said.

"The Death March?" said Ingrid.

"The Death March," said Mr. Sidney.

"So you and Grampy and Major Ferrand weren't on the Death March?" Ingrid said, trying to remember the details of the *Echo* article, at the same time beginning to suspect that Mr. Samuels hadn't got all of them right.

"Didn't say that, now did I?" said Mr. Sidney. Piggy came to the side of the pen, his twisted little tail vibrating. "Wanna fetch one of those Slim Jims, kid?"

Ty went to the shelf by the big doors, brought back a Slim Jim.

"Just toss it in," Mr. Sidney said. "Don't need to take off the wrapper – he's not fussy."

"Really?" said Ty, eyes lighting up.

"I'll take if off," Ingrid said. "It's no prob—"

Ty tossed in the Slim Jim. It disappeared in Piggy's mouth, wrapper and all.

"Hey," said Ty.

Mr. Sidney watched Piggy eat, his eyes growing vague again. "Would have killed for a Slim Jim," he said softly. After a silence he gave himself a little shake. "Where were we?"

"The Death March," Ingrid said.

Mr. Sidney nodded. "Death March," he said, and went silent again.

"Were the three of you on it, after all?" Ingrid said.

"Didn't say that, neither," Mr. Sidney said, coming to life. "We were on Corregidor, all right, but our unit got transferred to Bataan first day of April, reinforcing the line west of Limay." He licked his finger again, drew a line across the peninsula. "Next week, night of April six, that's when the enemy came through." His voice got quieter. "We couldn't stop 'em. Long time ago. Suppose that's one way of looking at it."

Did Grampy look at it that way? Ingrid didn't think so: he wouldn't even get in Mom's MPV, a Japanese car.

As though his mind had been running along the same lines, Mr. Sidney said, "Not the way your grandfather sees it, of course. Can't say as I blame him, after everything that happened."

"What happened?" Ty said.

Mr. Sidney gazed down at the rough map he'd drawn on the floor. "Hit us with these howitzers on Bataan – two-forties. Never want to hear them again. Plus they had planes and we didn't. No excuses. Buddies burned to a crisp in their foxholes – I saw that. The forest was on fire. Our company got trapped on a ridge, enemy on all sides. Surrounded is what I'm saying. We had a lot of Connecticut boys in the company, not sure why. Cyrus Ferrand – captain at the time – was in command. I was sergeant with the second platoon. Your grandfather was a corporal with the third. Best shot in the company, but that's not how he won his medal."

"How did he win his medal?" Ty said.

"Coming to that," said Mr. Sidney. "Don't rush me, kid. Should never have been on that ridge in the first place – Lieutenant Porterhouse of the first platoon told Ferrand we could never defend that damn ridge." Mr. Sidney shook his head.

"Not Mr. Porterhouse the gym teacher?" said Ingrid.

"His dad," said Mr. Sidney. "Died that night, up on

the ridge. Whole lot more would have, hadn't been for Aylmer."

"What did he do?" said Ty.

"Coming to that," said Mr. Sidney. "But first: there was only one way off that ridge, this trail down the south side – the high side. The enemy got a heavy machine gun going up there, firing down from above. We were doing all right, considering, dug in pretty good, but it didn't take much smarts to know that when the sun came up and they could see what they were doing, we'd be goners. We all knew it. Strangest feeling – waiting to die. That's when Aylmer took things into his own hands."

"How?" said Ty.

Mr. Sidney gave him a look. "I left out the noise," he said. "They were calling in the aircraft – didn't risk bombing us because of the chance of killing their own, so they strafed. Real noisy on the receiving end. Aylmer was right beside me, crouched down behind this tree trunk. He shouted something to me – didn't hear a word – and the next thing I knew, he took off."

"Took off?" said Ty.

This time Mr. Sidney didn't give him a look; in fact there was a new glow in his eyes. "Did he ever. Aylmer always could run, of course – high school state champ in the hundred-yard dash."

"He was?" said Ingrid.

Mr. Sidney nodded. "But he never ran faster than he did that night on the ridge. Ran right up to the machine-gun nest – all this in the dark, but a flare went off and I saw him like in a photograph, arm raised up, throwing a grenade. *Boom*. And then someone yelled, 'Go!' and we were all running, what was left of us, through that wiped-out machine-gun nest and down off the ridge, back behind our own lines. Point being, your grandfather saved a lot of lives that night."

"And that's why you'd do anything for him?" Ingrid said.

"Nope," said Mr. Sidney, spitting out a stray bit of cigar leaf. "Reason for that came later. But not much later. Would you believe it? Three days after that battle, we got orders to surrender."

"Who?" said Ty.

"All of us – all our fighting forces in Bataan, except for the ones on Corregidor. They held out a little longer. But the important thing is we didn't surrender. We were ordered to surrender." His eyes narrowed. "See the difference?"

Ingrid wasn't sure she did. Had they surrendered or not? But this felt like a good moment for keeping her mouth shut. And Mr. Sidney's next words cleared everything up.

"Very next morning they had us on the road to the prison camp. Not going to talk about the Death March – you can look it up. Not going to talk about the starvation, or the disease, the heat, or what happened to anybody who lagged behind, even to drink from a mud puddle."

"What happened to them?" said Ty.

"What did I just say?" said Mr. Sidney. "And drinking from the mud puddles turned out to be a bad idea anyway, even if you were dying of thirst, 'cause then you got a disease that most times was even quicker. That's what happened to me – so sick I couldn't stand up, let alone keep moving. But you had to keep moving, see? Because if you stopped—" Mr. Sidney drew his finger across his throat.

"How did you do it?" Ingrid said.

"I didn't," said Mr. Sidney. "Came a point where I just toppled over and lay in the dust, said my prayers."

"And then what?" said Ty.

"Then?" said Mr. Sidney. "Then Aylmer Hill picked me up and carried me on his back for three days." Ingrid felt Ty's hand on her knee, just for a moment. "Which is why," said Mr. Sidney, "if your grandfather's got a pig that needs looking after, then I'll be doing the looking after."

It went silent in the barn. Even the pig was still, watching. Mr. Sidney took a big puff from his cigar.

"Any questions?" he said.

"Where does the Coral Sea part come in?" Ty said.

Mr. Sidney took off his Battle of the Coral Sea cap, gazed at the writing. "No connection," he said.

"But you always wear it," said Ingrid.

Mr. Sidney nodded. "My brother Cedric fought in that," he said. "Petty officer second class on the *Sims*. Went to the bottom, May seventh, nineteen forty-two. Not that I knew at the time, me being in the camp and still plenty delirious."

"How long were you prisoners?" said Ingrid.

"Two and a half years."

"Two and a half years!" said Ty.

"Lucky to make it," said Mr. Sidney. "Lots didn't."

"But the three of you did," Ingrid said.

"What three?" said Mr. Sidney.

"You, Grampy, and Mr. Ferrand."

"Ferrand? When did I say anything about Ferrand?"

"That he was the commander," said Ingrid. "Up on the ridge."

"And then you all surrendered," said Ty.

"We were ord—" Mr. Sidney began.

"Ordered to surrender," Ty added quickly. "And after that came the Death March."

"Did I ever say Ferrand was on the Death March?"

"He wasn't?" Ingrid said.

"Nope. All the survivors from his company – fifty-nine men – but not him."

"How come?" Ingrid said.

"Don't know," said Mr. Sidney. "All I remember from the Death March is Aylmer's bloody footprints in the dust. Delirium – lasted for months."

"But didn't you and Grampy talk about it?" Ingrid said.

"Maybe, but nothing stuck. Word is Ferrand spent the rest of the war in London."

"London?" said Ingrid. "But you were all trapped in Bataan."

"Attached to staff headquarters or some such." Mr. Sidney rose. "Anyways, it's ancient history."

"Wow," said Ingrid, back home, Ty's room: Ty playing Madden, Ingrid sort of watching.

"Wow what? That double reverse?"

"No," said Ingrid. "Grampy. Think Mom and Dad know all that?"

"Mom and Dad – who cares?" said Ty, eyes on the screen. From that angle he looked a lot older. At that moment the secret of Grampy's illness was suddenly too much to bear. Ingrid opened her mouth, about to let it out, but before she could, Ty turned to her and said, "Know what I wish?" He'd never asked her a question like that before. "I wish I was older, old enough to go away to college."

"Don't say that," Ingrid said.

Ty didn't say anything. He ran another one of those double reverses. Grampy's secret stayed with Ingrid.

Later, Ingrid went looking for past editions of *The Echo*. She found the one she wanted in the blue recycling basket.

> *Even so long after the event, the Death March is not a subject Major Ferrand will talk about.*
>
> *"Time is a great healer," he says.*
>
> *How did the war change him? "We all grew up pretty fast," he says. He adds that lifelong friendships were formed, although he has not kept up with Mr. Sidney or Mr. Hill. Major Ferrand, a one-time racer on the ocean yacht circuit, describes himself as a "retired investor," and says he lives "very quietly now. It was all long ago."*

Ingrid remembered watching Grampy read that article, and how his eyes had turned so hard. She could see it clearly. Funnily enough, she could see him just as clearly – lit by a flare that had gone off half a century before her birth, about to hurl that grenade.

twenty-one

SNOW day, continued.

Mom was on a listing call – very important, as Ingrid, who'd heard a lot of real estate talk by now, knew well. It was all about getting listings: no listings, no power, inside the agency or out.

Ty was in his room, still playing video games; every once in a while Ingrid heard the crash of a helmet-to-helmet hit. She lay on her bed, turning pages in *The Complete Sherlock Holmes*, reading bits here and there.

Like "The Adventure of the Blue Carbuncle", for example, where the carbuncle – which turns out to be a diamond, although the definition Ingrid found in an online dictionary was "a boil full of pus" – is hidden in a goose. But what interested her now came before that, where Holmes and Watson are examining a black hat with a red silk lining for clues, and Watson says he can't see anything.

"On the contrary, Watson, you can see everything. You fail, however, to reason from what you see. You are

too timid in drawing your inferences."

Inferences? What were they, again? Ingrid looked the word up for the zillionth time. Okay. An inference came when you were on the receiving end of an implication, a word she now had a good grip on, thanks to Mr. Tulkinghorn. Point being, as Mr. Sidney would say, that red and black hat implied things to Holmes that Watson remained completely obliv—

Red and black. The combination sidetracked Ingrid, her mind shifting to the memory of Mr. Thatcher lying dead in his red-and-black-checked jacket. Someone killed him, not Grampy; but the murder weapon was a World War II–era Springfield sniper rifle and Grampy had been issued one, a rifle that was never returned. How old was Mr. Thatcher? Despite a superficial resemblance to Grampy – same size, same white hair – Mr. Thatcher had been a lot younger, maybe in his fifties, way too young for World War II. How could his death have anything to do with the war? Way off track. Mr. Thatcher was the conservation agent, maybe not that popular a job, so wouldn't the motive more likely be—

Ingrid heard a noise out back. The snowblower? Only Dad used the snowblower – strict rules about that. Was he here? She rose, went to the window. Not Dad but Grampy: Grampy in his red-and-black-checked jacket. He was clearing a path from the house to the path in the woods. How quickly he worked, just as fast as Dad, but why was he doing it in the first place?

In three or four minutes he'd reached the first trees. Then for some reason he kept going – Grampy, snowblower, and white curling plume all disappearing in the woods. The sound grew fainter and fainter, died away completely. Not long after that, Grampy returned, the snowblower now turned off. He pushed it into the garage, then reappeared with a wheelbarrow loaded with lumber and tools. Grampy followed the path, now clear, back into the woods. Ingrid went downstairs, put on her boots, hat, jacket, and mittens, and started up the path. She was barely in the woods before she heard hammering sounds.

Ingrid followed them to the tree house. Dad had built it when she and Ty were little; now it was pretty much wrecked. Until that steroid-ring business last fall, she hadn't been up there in years.

"Grampy?"

The hammering stopped. Grampy poked his head out the window, a pencil clamped between his teeth.

"What are you doing?" Ingrid said.

"Shoring up," said Grampy. "It's a disgrace."

"But we don't play here anymore."

"Who said anything about play?" He ducked back inside, and the hammering started up again.

Ingrid climbed the footholds Dad had nailed into the tree. The entrance was a round hole in the floor, twenty feet up. Ingrid pulled herself through. Inside was a small square room with a sign on one of the rotting boards: THE TREEHOUS. OWNR TY. ASISTENT INGRID. Grampy had already ripped out half a dozen of the old boards, was hammering new ones into place. He looked very energetic, not sick at all.

"Surprised you kids can't spell any better than that," he said.

"But that was years ago, Grampy."

He grunted, reached into his chest pocket for a nail.

"Grampy?"

"That's me."

"Why are you doing this?"

"Needs doing."

Ingrid took a chance. "Is it because of Dad?"

"What's he got to do with anything?" Grampy hammered furiously for a minute or two. "By the time he comes to his senses, the train'll be long gone."

"What train?" Ingrid said.

He didn't answer, maybe hadn't heard her over the hammering. After a while he stood back. "How's that look?"

"Much better."

"A fort's got to be defendable," Grampy said, "or else what's the point?"

"Defendable against what?" said Ingrid.

Grampy gazed out through the round window, a cold look in his eyes. Ingrid got a bad feeling. *Taking the plea deal didn't mean he would let them put him in jail.*

"Grampy," she said, "do you..."

He turned to her. "Spit it out."

"Do you have any ideas about who killed Mr. Thatcher?"

"Sure," said Grampy.

"Who?"

"Someone fed up with all his meddling. Isn't that obvious?"

"Who, for example?"

"Guy like that makes a lot of enemies. Could be most anybody."

She took another chance. "The thing is, Grampy, that's not true."

The expression in his eyes changed, but not toward annoyance or anger; more like puzzlement or confusion. She didn't like seeing him that way. "Oh?" he said.

"Because of the murder weapon," Ingrid said. "That's not the kind of rifle most anybody would have lying around."

"Suppose not."

"The World War Two Springfield with the sniper scope," Ingrid said.

"Yup," said Grampy.

"Can't be too many of them around."

"Nope."

"So I was wondering what happened to yours."

"Couldn't tell you," he said.

"Because you…?"

Now he did look annoyed. "What I said – couldn't tell you."

"Did you leave it behind?" Ingrid said.

"Leave it behind?"

"Up on that ridge." Grampy had charged the machine-gun nest with the grenade; had he been able to carry his rifle at the same time?

"Ridge?" he said. "What the hell are you talking about?"

Ingrid backed up a half step. "The ridge on Bataan, Grampy. Where you won the medal."

For a moment, Grampy went still. "How d'you know

about that?" he said, his voice much quieter.

"Mr. Sidney."

"Hole in his head," said Grampy.

"Meaning it's not true?"

Then something happened that surprised her – shocked her, really – and made her feel bad: Grampy's eyes filled with tears. Not just moistened or dampened, but filled with tears. He turned his back, faced the window.

Ingrid thought of putting her hand on his shoulder or something, decided not. Instead she said, "Ty and I would like to see the medal, Grampy."

Grampy turned back to her, eyes dry now, but he didn't look energetic anymore. "Wrong person got it," he said.

Right away Ingrid thought of Mr. Porterhouse's dad, the one who'd warned Major Ferrand – Captain Ferrand then – that they couldn't defend the ridge, and had ended up dying on it. "Who?" she said.

Grampy gazed at her as though making up his mind. He said, "My wife." For a moment Ingrid didn't understand; then she did. "Got into her bones," Grampy went on, "and back then they weren't so good at controlling pain, like now. She never complained, not a single time. Set an example."

Ingrid stepped forward, put her arms around Grampy. He patted her back. "Nothing to be upset about," he said, letting her go. "As for the rifle, it just disappeared."

"Disappeared?" she said.

"Night of the surrender," Grampy said. "Disappeared

right out of my tent. Had other things to think about at the time, of course, but what difference did it make? We had to give up our weapons anyway."

"Mr. Sidney says you didn't surrender – you were ordered to surrender."

"One thing he got right."

Ingrid still wasn't clear about the distinction, but something in Grampy's tone warned her off. "He also says Major Ferrand wasn't on the Death March."

That hard look that had appeared in Grampy's eyes when he read the *Echo* article on Major Ferrand? It was back. "Second thing he got right."

"Did Major Ferrand manage to get back to Corregidor before the surrender?" Ingrid said.

"Why d'you ask that?"

"Because the guys from Corregidor weren't on the Death March, so I thought that maybe…"

Grampy's head tilted, as though he wanted to see her from another angle. "You're a smart young woman," he said.

Woman? There was a first.

"But answer me this," Grampy said. "How can the commanding officer go one way while the rest of the company goes another?"

Ingrid didn't know.

"Maybe he lit out for Corregidor," Grampy said. "Maybe not."

"What do you mean?"

"Quite the sailor boy, Cyrus Ferrand," said Grampy.

"He was in the Navy?"

Grampy laughed. "You're a funny kid," he said. "I'm

going to mi—" He cut himself off, cleared his throat. "No, he was in the Army, but before the war he kept a yacht in Newport, did a lot of ocean racing."

"He had his yacht in Bataan?"

Grampy laughed again. "Don't know exactly what happened and how," he said, "but the intent – that I'm sure of."

Ingrid was lost. Maybe he saw that on her face.

"He disappeared that last night – missing in action, happened all the time. Later – this was in the camp – I ran into another POW who'd seen him casting off in a fishing boat just before dawn. Commandeered it, evidently."

"What does that mean?"

"Took it," said Grampy. "This POW saw some muzzle flashes."

"You mean he shot the fishermen?"

"No idea," said Grampy. "I assumed he'd been sunk by the enemy or lost at sea, but after the war, I found out he got picked up by a neutral freighter – Swedish maybe – in a matter of hours."

"So he deserted, Grampy?"

"Couldn't call it that," Grampy said. "A POW has a duty to try to escape."

"But you weren't POWs yet."

"That didn't bother me – got to be sensible," Grampy said. "He was the commanding officer – that's what bothered me."

"Did he take any of the men with him?" Ingrid said.

"Sixty-four-dollar question," said Grampy. "Nope."

"And he spent the rest of the war in London?"

"Staff job," said Grampy.

"Did you ever tell anybody?"

Grampy shook his head. "Long time ago."

"That's what everybody keeps saying – Mr. Sidney, Major Ferrand, and now you."

"Done some thinking on that, matter of fact," said Grampy. "Occurred to me maybe it wasn't a good idea to let Cyrus Ferrand just swan off to eternity."

"You're going to do something about it?"

"What I *was* going to do," said Grampy, "before all this ... this other—" He cut himself off, said, "Sh. Someone's coming."

They peered down from the tree house, the hammer not quite still in Grampy's hand. Ingrid heard soft thudding, faint and rhythmic. She saw a lone figure on the path – a snowshoeing figure, moving in the direction of her house.

"Joey?"

He stopped, looked up, approached the tree house. "Hi," he said. "Snow day."

"Joey, this is my grandfather."

"Um," said Joey. "Sir."

Grampy made a little gesture with the hammer.

"Ingrid?" Joey said.

"Yeah?"

"Snow day."

"I know."

"So I was thinking – maybe she wants to go snowshoeing again."

"Who are we talking about?" Ingrid said.

Joey looked surprised. "You. Ingrid."

Ingrid thought she heard Grampy chuckle, very softly.

At that moment, she got an idea, maybe a pretty good one. "Okay," she said.

They snowshoed through the woods. Joey wasn't going fast this time, in fact seemed to be making an effort to stay beside her.

"You're allowed to talk to me now?" Ingrid said.

"Not, um," said Joey.

She took that for a no; meaning the plea deal hadn't happened yet. "Your dad know you're here?"

"We're not going to talk about the case."

"But does he?"

"He went to work early."

"So he doesn't?"

Joey stopped, faced her. "We're not going to talk about the case."

"Fine," said Ingrid. "But there's something I want you to do."

Joey looked wary. "About the case?"

"No," Ingrid said. "This is about Nigel." She told him the whole story.

"You think this private eye from Bridgeport stole Nigel?"

"But not for himself," Ingrid said. "For a client."

"Who?" said Joey.

"That's what I want you to find out."

"Me?" said Joey.

"Your dad knows Dieter Meinhof," Ingrid said. "He recognized his car."

"So?"

"So Dieter Meinhof's been in Echo Falls before. That

means he had some client here in the past. I want to know who."

"But why would it be the same one as now?" said Joey.

"Might not be," Ingrid said. "Got a better idea?"

They walked in silence for a while. It was a three-colored world – white snow, brown trees, gray sky – a bleak world, but they had it to themselves. *Kids on their own.*

"Okay," said Joey. "I'll do it."

twenty-two

knock on the door.

Ingrid looked out, saw an SUV in the driveway, the one with that LEAGLE plate. A plow roared down Maple Lane; the sky was clear. She opened up.

"Hello, Iris," said Mr. Tulkinghorn. Iris? Weren't lawyers supposed to get the facts straight, step one? "Your grandfather in?"

"He's sleeping," Ingrid said.

Mr. Tulkinghorn gazed down at her; she could feel him thinking. He'd acquired a nice suntan since the last time she'd seen him. "Can I trust you to do something for me?"

Ingrid nodded.

"Make sure he gets this." Mr. Tulkinghorn held out a manila envelope. "Have him go over the contents and call if he's got any questions."

Ingrid took the envelope.

"Call by close of day, that is," said Mr. Tulkinghorn. "The signing's tomorrow, ten a.m. Can you remember all that for me?"

"He gets the envelope," Ingrid said. "He goes over the contents, calls by close of day if there are questions. Signing's tomorrow, ten a.m."

Mr. Tulkinghorn blinked.

Ingrid took the envelope into the house, carried it upstairs. She stood outside the closed office door. "Grampy? Grampy?" No answer.

She went into her room, sat at her desk, examined the envelope. *Aylmer Hill: Personal and Confidential.* Steaming envelopes open, a familiar concept: She could see herself holding this one over a kettle, a sneaky expression on her face. Instead of all that, Ingrid slid her thumb under the seal and just tore it open.

Inside were pages and pages of dense print, the sentences so complicated, beyond her. But the Post-it note stuck to the top of page one was clear: FYI – plea agreement, final draft. At ten a.m. tomorrow Grampy would be convicted of manslaughter and on his way to jail – unless he was getting ready to do something really crazy in the tree house. Ingrid heard footsteps in the hall, stuck the envelope in the top drawer of her desk.

Ty came in. "Phone," he said. He tossed it to her and went away.

"Sorry," Joey said.

"You couldn't find out?" Ingrid said.

"I tried."

"Thanks."

"My dad doesn't know," Joey said. "Like, who the client was."

"I get it," Ingrid said.

"But he's from here," Joey said. "Originally."

"Who is?"

"The private eye. Dieter Meinhof."

"He's from Echo Falls?"

"Yeah," said Joey. "His mom's a housekeeper for this old rich guy who's hardly ever around."

"What old rich guy?"

"Something Ferrand."

"He's one of the Ferrands?"

"You don't have to yell at me."

"Cyrus?"

"Yeah. That was it."

"Dieter Meinhof's mother works for the Ferrands?"

"Mrs. Meinhof's a real witch, my dad says. They were all afraid of her when they were kids." A real witch: Ingrid was pretty sure she'd seen her before – with Major Ferrand at Moo Cow, having a bad reaction to Ingrid's Special.

Years ago, Ingrid and Chloe Ferrand – daughter of Tim, Dad's boss at the Ferrand Group – had been good friends. But in seventh grade, Chloe had left the Echo Falls public school system, switching to Cheshire Country Day instead, and now they didn't see each other much. Plus in the fall a couple of things had happened – like Ingrid winning the lead role in the *Alice in Wonderland* production when Chloe thought she had it in the bag – that had strained what was left of their connection. So this wasn't going to be easy.

Ingrid dialed Chloe's number.

"Hey, Chloe, how are you doing?"

Pause. "Who is this?"

"Ingrid."

Silence.

"Snow day," said Ingrid. "Here, at least. You too?"

"I suppose," said Chloe. "I wasn't going to school today anyway."

"No?"

"No."

More silence.

"How come?"

"I had a shoot. But of course it got canceled too."

"A shoot?"

"Photo shoot," said Chloe.

"Oh," Ingrid said. Chloe was the most beautiful thirteen-year-old girl in Echo Falls, maybe in the entire central state, already had some real professional modeling gigs. "Too bad."

"I don't care," said Chloe. "I wasn't in the mood."

What kind of mood did you have to be in for a photo shoot? Ingrid wanted to know – not that she'd ever have any practical use for the information – but this wasn't the time. "So," she said, "a free day."

"I guess."

"What are you up to?"

"Not much."

"Want to come over?" Ingrid said; the least sincere invitation of her whole life.

"To your place?" said Chloe. Would anyone living in splendor on an estate like Ferrands', with its indoor pool among other things, want to spend the day at

99 Maple Lane? Maybe, but not Chloe.

"Yeah," said Ingrid. "We could go snowshoeing."

"Excuse me?"

"In the woods."

"What for?"

"What for?"

"Why would I want to do that?"

"I get it," said Ingrid. "Like when you could be swimming in your indoor pool instead."

Pause. "Actually," said Chloe, "a swim sounds nice."

"Doesn't it?" Ingrid said and waited. And waited and waited, knowing that unless she kept her mouth shut, she'd blow it. She realized for the first time what a weapon silence could be.

At last, Chloe said, "I suppose you could come over here."

"Thanks, Chloe. Sounds great."

"For a little while," said Chloe; or something like that – Ingrid, already hanging up, didn't quite hear.

The Ferrands' estate stood on a hill by the river, acres and acres with a huge main house, guesthouses, and other outbuildings, three or four miles from 99 Maple Lane. No one to drive her – Grampy asleep, and not allowed out in any case, Mom at work, Dad not in the picture. Ingrid stuffed a bathing suit and towel in her backpack, called out, "Going to Chloe's," as she passed Ty's room, and went outside. Maple Lane to Hillcrest, Hillcrest to Crestview, Crestview to River: she was learning Echo Falls. But as Ingrid left the house, she happened to glance down the street, not in the direction of Hillcrest but toward Avondale, and saw a woman trying to stick a sign into the McGreevys' snow-covered lawn.

Ingrid walked down the street. The sign, from Valley Properties, Riverbend's big rival, read: FOR SALE – NEW LISTING.

"Hi," Ingrid said.

The woman turned. "Does that look straight?"

"Yeah," said Ingrid. "She's, um, they're, um, moving?"

"Yes," said the woman. "Isn't it a lovely little home?"

What about the leaky basement? Ingrid kept that fact to herself. "Where?" she said.

"Where?" said the woman.

"Where's she moving to?"

"Boston."

"Boston?"

"I think that's where she's from." A cell phone rang. The woman fumbled in her purse. Ingrid drifted away.

She climbed the broad staircase leading up to the huge black double doors at Chloe's house – biggest house in Echo Falls – and knocked, the tip of her nose feeling numb from the cold. The maid answered. She wore a plain gray dress and a white apron and carried a beautiful Chinese vase filled with delicate crimson flowers of a kind Ingrid had never seen.

"Hi," said Ingrid.

"You are for Chloe?" said the maid, the *y* sounding a little like a *j*.

Against, thought Ingrid at once, but she just said, "Yes."

"This way."

The maid led Ingrid down a long hall lined with paintings, around a corner, and left her at the pool room. The pool room was high ceilinged, glassed in on three sides, almost as big as Ingrid's whole house; the pool itself was a replica of one in Pompeii or someplace, overhung with a blazing chandelier that had come all the way from France. Chloe lay reading on a chaise longue, fully clothed.

"Sorry, Ingrid," she said. "I forgot."

"Forgot what?"

She rotated her wrist slowly, half extended her index finger in the direction of the pool. Ingrid looked: no water.

"Some – I don't know – maintenance issue?" Chloe said.

Ingrid sat on the adjoining chaise. "That's all right," she said. "What are you reading?"

Chloe angled the cover so Ingrid could see: *The Supermodel Way of Life.*

Ingrid laughed, assuming it was some kind of satire.

"What's funny?"

Too late she remembered the whole photo-shoot business, a little hard to reconcile with how smart Chloe was, a straight-A student at CCD, where they didn't give them away. "Nothing," Ingrid said. "Any good?"

"It has some insights."

"Like?"

Chloe raised an eyebrow, an elegantly curved golden

eyebrow. "I'll lend it to you when I'm finished," she said.

That was cutting, but so quick and sharp Ingrid couldn't have said exactly how. She got up, went to the tall window, looked out. The Ferrands' land sloped down toward the river, other buildings standing here and there, some of them quite big, like normal houses. Smoke rose from the chimney of one of them, more of a cottage, maybe, wood shingled and half hidden in a grove of trees, close to the river. More than a grove, in fact: the trees covered a gradual rise to the left – south? – of the cottage, all the way to the top and beyond.

"Are those trees part of the town woods?" Ingrid said.

Chloe rose, came over. "Don't think so," she said. "Aren't they ours?"

They stood side by side – Chloe much taller – gazing out the window. What did Chloe see? Ingrid didn't know; same world, she suspected, but two different takes.

"Who lives in the cottage?" she said.

Chloe turned, the look on her face as close as she ever came to surprise. "How did you know we called it that?" she said. "The Cottage?"

"I didn't."

"That's what I like about you, Ingrid."

"What?"

"You're intuitive."

"I am?"

"Guess that disproves it," Chloe said. Then, for a moment, they were laughing together, like good friends.

"My great-uncle Cyrus lives there when he's around, which isn't often."

"What's he like?"

Chloe shrugged. "An old man. Hardly ever comes up to the house."

"He was in *The Echo*."

"You read *The Echo*?"

"Yeah," Ingrid said. "It was about him and the war."

"Wasn't he some kind of hero?" said Chloe.

"Some kind," Ingrid said.

A man spoke behind them. "Chloe?"

They turned. Tim Ferrand stood on the other side of the pool, wearing jeans and a sweater. Ingrid had never seen him casually dressed; he looked smaller, and also like he was wearing borrowed clothes, even though they fit fine.

"Is that you, Ingrid?" he said.

"Hi, Mr. Ferrand."

"Haven't seen you in a while," he said. "How..." His eyes shifted. "How are things at home?"

Ingrid felt her chin tilting up in that defiant way it sometimes had and the reply *None of your business* struggling to get out. "Good," Ingrid said.

For a moment it looked like Mr. Ferrand was going to ask a follow-up. Instead he spoke to Chloe. "Can you get ready?" he said. "We're going up to Stowe."

"What about school?" Chloe said.

"Tomorrow's Friday," Mr. Ferrand said. "We'll take the weekend. I forget – do you ski, Ingrid?"

"No."

"You would have been welcome to come. We'll drop you on the way."

"That's all right," Ingrid said, feeling the pull of The Cottage behind her, like a magnet. "I can walk."

"Don't be silly," said Mr. Ferrand.

Mr. Ferrand drove, Ingrid and Chloe in back. No skis on the roof, or anything like that: All the equipment waited at the Ferrands' Stowe chalet.

"How long does it take?" said Ingrid, just to make conversation, be polite.

"No idea," said Chloe.

"An hour, depending," said Mr. Ferrand.

"I thought it was farther."

"We go with Nevin," Chloe said.

"Who's Nevin?"

"Our pilot," Chloe said.

"Oh," said Ingrid; conversations with Chloe often ended like that, Ingrid reduced to *oh*.

They dropped her in front of 99 Maple Lane. Getting dark already: Long shadows blackened the street, and the western sky was fiery. She noticed that the TT was in the driveway. What was that about? No time to investigate. The moment the Ferrands' car was out of sight, Ingrid started walking back to Chloe's.

twenty-three

it was almost fully dark by the time Ingrid got back to the Ferrands' house – an enormous silhouette against a deep-purple sky – and much colder. The tall gates to the driveway were closed, but Ingrid, ninety-seven pounds, squeezed between the black bars, no problem. The packed-down snow in the driveway squeaked under her boots, the way it did when the temperature fell into single digits. Her whole face was numb now, and her toes too; her fingers, balled up inside her wool mittens, were still okay.

Halfway up the driveway a plowed lane led on a diagonal to the left, away from the house. Lights shone in a few windows, spilled over the snow, but didn't quite reach Ingrid. She followed the plowed lane across the Ferrands' vast property, past the outdoor pool and cabana, past the guesthouses, all dark. In the distance, way down the long slope, she could just see a curve of the river, iced over and glazed with the last light of sunset. Then the lane entered the woods – maybe the

Ferrands', maybe the town's – and the river vanished. Darkness spread around her, flowing silently through the trees. The only sounds were the squeaking of her boots in the packed snow and her own breathing, low and rapid. Ingrid tried to slow it down.

A light twinkled up ahead, disappeared, came again. Not long after that, she smelled smoke. The twinkle grew stronger, became a glow, and all at once Ingrid heard the raised voice of a woman, not far off. She sounded angry.

"Bad, bad, very bad. Bad." And then: *crack*. A single sharp whip-cracking sound.

Ingrid went still. She heard a door close, and the glow vanished. Silence. After a while she took another step: *squeak*. Almost at once, a door opened and slammed shut. Then headlights flashed on, up ahead and partly obscured by trees, but pointing right at her. Ingrid dove off the lane, rolled behind a thick tree trunk, snow getting down her neck. The headlights drew closer and a car went by, the hawk-nosed woman at the wheel, her face green in the dashboard lights. A minute or so later the taillights disappeared somewhere toward the main road, and the engine sounds faded. Ingrid rose, brushed off the snow, returned to the path, kept going: *squeak, squeak,* but nothing she could do about it.

The lane curved toward the right and The Cottage appeared, trees dense all around like a single organism, heavy branches reaching down to the roof. Sparks flew up the chimney, but The Cottage was dark except for a single faint light in a downstairs window. Ingrid stepped into the small yard – the backyard, she realized, from the woodpile and chopping block. What was that? A whining sound? She listened hard. Some animal in the woods? Just the wind? The sound stopped before she could make up her mind.

But the wind was rising, no doubt about that: It reached up between the hems of her pant legs and her boot tops, all icy. A branch scratched at the roof. *Kids on their own.*

Ingrid moved across the yard. The moon blinked through the treetops, made tiny reflections of itself on the silvery parts of a snowmobile parked by the house. She came to the window where the light showed, stood on her tiptoes, peered in.

Data: a small kitchen, lit only by an old-fashioned oil lamp on the table. Beside the lamp sat a fruit basket. A cloud of fruit flies hovered over it. What else? Stove, fridge, cupboards, a wall calendar with a picture of a cemetery. And on the floor in one corner stood a tin bowl, the kind dogs drank from. She thought she heard that whine again. Was it coming from somewhere inside? Ingrid held her breath, listened hard, heard nothing.

No cars around, one little light left on, not the usual time for sleeping: therefore no one home, pure logic. This was her chance. What was that expression? *Window of opportunity.* Ingrid decided to take it literally. She pressed the heels of her hands against the top part of one of those wooden frames – mullions? – that held in the window panes, and pushed up. The window didn't budge.

She moved a few steps away to the back door. People sometimes kept an extra key hidden under a flowerpot or the doormat, or up on the sill above the door; Mr. Rubino had rigged a setup involving a hidden button and a key that came popping out of the wall cuckooclock style. The Cottage had no flowerpot and the sill was too high. Ingrid looked under the mat – a mat that said *Willkommen* – and found nothing. She rose, put her face to the round window in the door, saw shadows and gloom. Then that whine came again, for sure this time: the sound seemed to vibrate in the glass. Ingrid's hand went to the doorknob. She turned it, in the unlikely event—

The door opened. A little jolt went through her; not fear, exactly. It was more like: *This is meant to be.* Ingrid glanced back, saw nothing but the woods and, in the distance, the lights of the Ferrands' house. She stepped into The Cottage and closed the door softly behind her.

The Cottage was vague and shadowy inside, full of dark shapes that all seemed about to move. Ingrid saw a faint glow to her left, followed it down a short hall, ended up in a small sitting room furnished with a few pieces of severe-looking furniture. The glow came from a fire burning low in the fireplace. Above the fireplace hung the mounted head of some kind of animal – a wild sheep, maybe – with long curving horns. Its huge eyes reflected the firelight; they looked terrified.

Ingrid heard the whining sound again. It seemed to come right from the sheep head, almost made her jump. At that point parts of her, maybe led by her feet, had had enough. They tried to take over, race her right out of that room, out of The Cottage, all the way back home. Ingrid got a grip, mastered those rebellious parts, and merely backed away into the hall.

She walked by the back door, glancing out the round window and seeing only the night. Next came a closed door. Ingrid put her ear to it. Silence. Slow and cautious, she turned the knob, pushed the door open, found herself in the kitchen. The fruit on the table was all rotten. She waved her hand at the hovering fruit flies and they vanished.

Ingrid went to the corner, crouched down by the dog bowl. Empty. She took off her mitten and ran her finger along the bottom, felt dampness. And what was this? Clinging to her fingertip, a single dog hair.

She examined it by the light of the old-fashioned oil lamp: a thick sort of hair, dark brown in color. Nigel wasn't exactly dark brown in color: He had a tweedy coat, like a Scottish heath, Mom had said, whatever that was. Could a dark brown hair like this be part of his tweedy coat? Ingrid didn't know. She was still thinking about that when she heard the whining sound again. Where was it coming from? She saw another door leading from the kitchen, with stairs rising beyond it.

Ingrid took the oil lamp and climbed the stairs. At the top she found a bathroom flanked by two bedrooms, each with a low ceiling and a narrow bed. One had a dressing table with a mirror, hairbrush, and framed photograph of a smiling Dieter Meinhof with his arm around the hawk-nosed woman. She had wild hair and was showing her teeth, although it couldn't be called smiling. *Mrs. Meinhof's a real witch. They were all afraid of her when they were kids.*

Sailing photographs hung on the walls of the second

bedroom, huge ocean yachts with Cyrus Ferrand at the helm in every one. Half a dozen trophies stood on a desk. Ingrid picked one up: MAJOR CYRUS FERRAND: CHAMPION.

She opened the top drawer, saw a check lying on a bunch of papers. Ingrid held the check to the light: a check to Cyrus Ferrand from Bank of America dated the day before for $1,243,799.54; an attached Post-it note read: *Quarterly Dividends*. Ingrid was replacing it when she noticed a newspaper clipping in the back of the drawer. She pulled it out.

Not one clipping but three, stapled together at the top left-hand corner, all from *The Echo*. Ingrid was familiar with each one: CONSERVATION AGENT FOUND MURDERED; ARREST IN THE DEATH OF CONSERVATION AGENT; MURDER WEAPON IDENTIFIED. What interested her now were the comments and markings she saw in the margins, red-pen comments and markings in a spiky hand that pressed hard, sometimes poking right through the paper.

In the margin of CONSERVATION AGENT FOUND MURDERED, beside the line about the identity of the victim and the location of the body, were the words *DAMN IT TO HELL!* Was this Cyrus Ferrand's writing? Ingrid pawed through the drawer, discovered his signature on a letter to some stockbroker: his writing, no question. Had Cyrus Ferrand known Mr. Thatcher? Had they been friends? How else to explain his reaction to the news?

On the second clipping – ARREST IN THE DEATH OF CONSERVATION AGENT – beside Grampy's picture, he'd written only this: *??*

And on the third – MURDER WEAPON IDENTIFIED – there were three red exclamation marks: *!!!* They came at the bottom of the article, just after this sentence: *Mr. Hill was issued a Springfield rifle of that type during World War II and Army records contain no evidence that he ever returned it.*

!!!

Ingrid folded the clippings with care and put them into her jacket pocket. They were evidence, links in a chain. But evidence of what? *Think, Griddie, think.* But no thoughts came, not even the feeblest little notion.

And then came the whine again, very faint, almost inaudible; but rising from somewhere below.

Ingrid closed the drawer and left the room, carrying the oil lamp. She went downstairs and in that back hall, outside the kitchen, saw something hanging on a hook, something long and thin with a leather grip that she hadn't noticed before. For a moment or two she didn't know what it was. And then she did: a whip. The lash hung down, the last ten or twelve inches coiling on the floor.

It wasn't particularly cold in The Cottage, but all at once Ingrid felt colder than she had outside; her teeth even chattered a little. The whine? Yes, once more, rising from below, beyond doubt. Ingrid walked down the hall, came to another door. She opened it, held out the oil lamp. Its light, not strong, drove the shadows back a few feet, revealing a rough, unfinished staircase, steeply descending.

Ingrid went down, down to a damp-smelling basement with an earthen floor, cement-block walls, and big shadowy shapes like furnaces and hot water heaters. The light from the oil lamp gleamed dully on a metal ring in the far wall. She went closer, her little light pushing at the gloom, revealing a thick chain attached to the ring, hanging down to the floor, just enough chain to reach—

Oh, no.

Just enough chain to hook onto the collar of a dog, lying in a pool of darkness; not enough chain to let him lower his head quite to the floor.

"Nigel!"

She fell to her knees beside him, set the lamp on the floor. He looked up at her, his big brown eyes full of some unhappy story he could never tell.

"Poor Nigel." She patted him. He thumped his tail on the floor, but just once, and not hard at all. How skinny he was! And what was this? Something over his face? A ... a muzzle?

A muzzle. Anger surged through her. Ingrid was angrier than she'd ever been in her life, shaking with it. She tore off the muzzle, flung it across the room, and went to work on the chain with trembling fingers, trying to unfasten it from Nigel's collar. At that moment a door opened up above, and footsteps sounded on the floorboards.

twenty-four

ingrid went still, but Nigel did not. His whole body started shaking. Ingrid stroked him, at the same time trying to get that chain off his collar. The footsteps moved overhead, shoe heels landing hard. Overhead might be the kitchen. Uh-oh – whoever it was might notice that—

Ingrid heard a voice, quite clearly, a woman's voice from above. Voices carried through walls and floors like that at Grampy's, too, not much insulation in old houses. The woman said, "Strange. Didn't I leave a...?"

Silence.

An oil lamp; and there it was, on the floor beside Ingrid. She pushed it closer to Nigel, worked frantically at the chain, hooked to his collar in some difficult way. Why wouldn't it come—

The chain came free; came free, all right, but swung slowly back toward the cement-block wall. Ingrid grabbed at it, just missing. The chain struck the wall, with a sound somewhere between a thud and a clang.

But not very loud, surely not carrying as far as—

More movement above, quicker now. The woman, her voice rising – not at all a musical voice – called, "Fritz?"

Fritz? Who was Fritz?

The woman spoke again, her tone now sugary in a sickening sort of way, "Are you misbehaving down there, Fritzie? Must I remind you what happens to bad dogs?"

Nigel whined, a whimpering, helpless sound. Ingrid never would have thought him capable of a sound like that. "Sh," she said, very quietly.

"You know how I hate that wretched whining," the woman called. After that a pause; Nigel's ears pricked up just a little, as though waiting to hear something. And then it came: *crack!* – that sharp explosive kind of crack made only by a whip. Nigel cringed.

A light went on at the top of the stairs. He cringed some more. A shadow, the shadow of a big woman, loomed down the stairs. Ingrid glanced around, saw a door behind her. She picked up the oil lamp, opened the door: not a door to the outside and escape, but a deep storage room, full of junk. A hard heel clacked on the top stair.

There was nowhere else to go. Ingrid stepped into the storage room. "Nigel." She breathed the name. He heard her – she could see that in his eyes – but was too scared to move. Ingrid put down the lamp, hurried to Nigel, took him by the collar, and dragged him inside. As she closed the door, she heard those hard footsteps coming down.

Ingrid noticed a space between the bottom of the door and the floor, wide enough for light to leak out. She turned, lowered her head over the lamp, about to blow out the flame. As she did, her gaze fell on an object standing in the corner: a rifle. And not just any rifle, but an old-fashioned-looking rifle with a brown wooden stock and a skinny black scope mounted on the top, just like the one in the picture Mr. Tulkinghorn had showed her. Was this the Springfield sniper gun that had vanished from Grampy's tent on the night of the surrender of Bataan, the same night Cyrus Ferrand had made his escape on a commandeered fishing boat? The gun Grampy had never returned, because he no longer had it? The gun that now, so many years later, had been used to murder Mr. Thatcher? But why? Why would Cyrus Ferrand want to kill the conservation agent? Had Mr. Thatcher been bothering the Ferrands, too? Wouldn't the Ferrands, with all the lawyers they could afford, end up getting their own way like they always—

"Now we will discover what happens to whining dogs."

Ingrid blew out the light. For a few moments she was completely blind, down in the basement storage room of The Cottage, Nigel quivering beside her.

"Fritz?"

Ingrid heard a soft click, the kind made by a switch, and a ribbon of light appeared under the closet door. More footsteps, muffled on the dirt floor. "What is going—?" Chain links clanked together. Pause. Then: "How did such a stupid animal manage to— What is this? Your muzzle? Bad. Bad. Very bad."

Footsteps approached. Nigel shook harder. *Sh, sh.* Ingrid didn't say that out loud, of course, didn't even breathe it this time, just thought *sh* with all her might, hoping the thought would leap somehow into Nigel's head, keep him quiet.

The toes of two shoes appeared in the ribbon of light under the door – not shoes, more like boots, black leather boots with pointy ends. The voice came again, right outside. "You have a friend, perhaps?" Ingrid heard a strange scratching sound, maybe the woman running her fingernail over the door. She pressed her hand on Nigel's back, thought, *sh, sh, oh please sh.* Another pause, this one longer. "And the lamp? What dog can make off with a burning lamp?"

The pointy toes crept back, out of sight. Footsteps retreated. The woman was thinking about that lamp; Ingrid could feel it. Thoughts like: where was it? did she really leave it on the table? or maybe somewhere else? A boot heel came down on a wooden stair. The woman was on her way back up. She was going to double-check, and that would take a minute or two, maybe enough time to find a window and—

From out of the blue – and for no good reason at this, of all moments, when things were actually starting to look a bit better – Nigel let out a long, high-rising whine, real loud, pretty close to a howl, the kind you could hear from miles away. Ingrid clamped her hand over his mouth, but way too late, and in the process she knocked over the lamp, which shattered all over the place, filling the air with an oily smell.

Silence. A terrible silence that built and built, like a

balloon that kept on inflating. And then: *crack!* The sound froze Ingrid like a figure in a nightmare. She knew she had to move, try to run, do something right now this very second or it would be too late, but she just couldn't. The closet door flew open.

Light flooded in, blinding her for a moment. And in that moment a long-nailed hand reached into the closet and pulled her out by the hair.

Ingrid tumbled onto the basement floor. Her vision cleared. Mrs. Meinhof stood over her, whip in hand, eyes hard and angry.

"Who are you?" she said. "How dare you break into my house?"

Ingrid tried to wriggle away. Mrs. Meinhof followed. "I want my dog," Ingrid said.

"Your dog?"

Ingrid twisted around, looking for Nigel. He was cowering in the storage room.

"That?" Mrs. Meinhof said. "That is not your dog. It is mine." She stared down at Ingrid. Recognition dawned in her eyes. "I know who you are," she said, "The thief who stole him from me last fall, stole him and spoiled him."

"That's not true," Ingrid said. "I found him."

"Liar."

"And you don't deserve him anyway," Ingrid said. "I'm taking him home."

"Never."

"Or..." said Ingrid, an idea on the way.

"Or?"

"Or I'll report you."

"Report me?"

"Yes," said Ingrid. "For the way you treat him."

The woman's eyes shifted.

Ingrid realized she was on to something, pushed the idea a little farther. "Why don't you call the police?"

"The police?"

"To arrest me for breaking in."

Mrs. Meinhof's eyes shifted again. Then came a surprise: she pulled a cell phone from the pocket of her long black skirt. Mrs. Meinhof thought the police would be on her side? That had to mean she didn't know that the murder weapon in the Thatcher case was just a few feet away. And that was where Ingrid would begin, with the murder weapon, the second the police walked in.

The woman punched some numbers on her cell phone: more than the three required for 911. That fact was just striking Ingrid when the woman spoke: "Dieter? Come at once."

Ingrid heard a tiny voice on the other end. "Now, Mother? I'm kind of—"

"At once, do you hear? We have prob—"

Ingrid didn't wait to hear more. She rolled away, sprang to her feet, ran toward the stairs. "Nigel!"

He didn't budge, stayed exactly where he was, trembling deep in the storage room. Ingrid wheeled around, raced in, and grabbed him. And just as she had him in her arms, she heard another *crack*, a whip crack like the others, only this time she felt a horrible red-hot pain across her shoulders, even through the padding of her jacket.

Ingrid fell to the floor. The whip cracked again, just

missing, raising dust inches from her face. At that a complete change came over Nigel. He growled and the hairs on his back rose straight up, his chest swelling to twice normal size. Then he charged straight at Mrs. Meinhof. She spun toward him, raising the whip, but not in time. Nigel sank his teeth into her leg and clamped on.

Mrs. Meinhof screamed in pain, a bloodcurdling scream like she was about to die. Ingrid dove across the closet and grabbed that gun, Grampy's old Springfield. Bigger and heavier than his .22, the one he'd taught her to shoot, but how different could it be? She found the safety, flicked it off. Mrs. Meinhof flailed at Nigel with the whip, but he wouldn't let go.

Ingrid pointed the gun at her.

"Don't move," she said.

Mrs. Meinhof froze. "You wouldn't."

"I would," Ingrid said. "Now drop that whip."

Mrs. Meinhof hesitated. Ingrid's trigger finger, all by itself, started to squeeze. Could she really do it? The expression in Mrs. Meinhof's eyes changed, showed real fear. She dropped the whip.

"Come, Nigel," Ingrid said.

Nigel let go of Mrs. Meinhof's leg and came, but on his way did something amazing. He ducked his head and scooped up the whip, bringing it with him.

"Good boy," Ingrid said.

His tail wagged. Nigel wasn't stupid; everybody was wrong about that. His mind just worked in its own way.

Keeping the gun on Mrs. Meinhof, Ingrid walked out of the storage room, Nigel right beside her. She stepped sideways along the wall, past Mrs. Meinhof, toward the stairs.

"Get in," she said, pointing the gun muzzle at the storage room.

Mrs. Meinhof hesitated. Ingrid raised the barrel an inch or two. Mrs. Meinhof limped into the storage room.

"Close the door."

The door closed. No bolt or key or anything to lock it with, but this was good enough: in seconds Ingrid would be out in the darkness, safe and on her way home. She took the whip from Nigel and dropped it into the gap under one of the stairs, out of sight.

Ingrid climbed up, Nigel beside her. She glanced back at the storage room: door closed. Yes, safe and on her way home, and more than that, she had evidence: not just the murder weapon, but those three clippings from *The Echo*. They were evidence too, links in a chain that she was sure told the real story of the murder, if only she could fit it all together. That meant understanding what Cyrus Ferrand had written in the margins.

DAMN IT TO HELL! beside the article about the murder of Mr. Thatcher.

?? beside the notice of Grampy's arrest.

!!! beside the identification of the murder weapon.

Meaning? Didn't it mean that Cyrus Ferrand was upset about the murder of Mr. Thatcher, confused about Grampy's arrest, and excited by the identification of the weapon? And therefore? She didn't know. Something, another link maybe, was missing. Then, just as she topped the last stair and entered the hall, heading for the back door, that missing link started to come, in the shape of a fact she already knew: those two red-and-black-checked jackets, one Grampy's, the other Mr. Thatcher's. Add in the related facts of both men's snowy-white hair and similar size. From a distance – a sniper's distance – it would be easy to mistake one for the other.

Meaning? As Ingrid turned the knob on the back door, it hit her: far from being the murderer, Grampy was the target, the intended victim. She opened the door. But why would—

"And where do you think you're going?"

Dieter Meinhof was coming toward her across the yard, his sedan with the mudded-out plates parked on the other side. Ingrid pointed the rifle at him.

"Stop," she said.

He kept coming.

"I'm a good shot," Ingrid said. "My grandfather taught me."

He stopped.

"Hands up," Ingrid said.

Dieter raised his hands.

"Back up to the car."

Dieter backed up. Ingrid walked toward the lane, Nigel at her side, forcing herself not to run, to stay calm. Then the passenger door of the car opened, and Cyrus Ferrand stepped out.

"You're embarrassing yourself, Dieter," he said. "It's not loaded."

Ingrid turned on Cyrus Ferrand – a coward and a murderer. He moved closer, slow and calm, but there was something sick and dangerous in that one eye. Could she really do it? Oh, yes. There was lots of Grampy in her. She pulled the trigger.

Click.

Too late, she heard Mrs. Meinhof behind her and, a split second later, felt icy fingers close around her neck, amazingly strong.

"Run," Ingrid said.

For once Nigel did as he was told, taking off into the night.

twenty-five

"**found** these in her pocket," said Dieter
Meinhof, handing Cyrus Ferrand the *Echo* clippings.

They were in the living room of The Cottage – Cyrus
in a chair beneath the head of the wild sheep, the
Springfield rifle leaning against the wall; Dieter standing beside him; Ingrid sitting on the floor, hands tied in
front of her with a rope; Mrs. Meinhof nearby, casually
holding the free end. Cyrus glanced at the clippings
with his good eye. Then his head turned, and that eye
fastened on Ingrid.

"Mind explaining again what you're doing here?" he
said.

"I told you," Ingrid said. "I came for my dog."

"We've established that the dog is not yours," Cyrus
said. He held up the clippings. "What is your interest in
these?"

*Careful, Griddie. He has to keep thinking this is
about Nigel, and only Nigel.* "They're about my grandfather," she said.

"I'm aware of that," he said. "But why—" Cyrus stopped himself, his gaze going to Dieter and Mrs. Meinhof. Both of them were looking at the clippings in a mystified sort of way, as though … as though they were really interested in the answer. And therefore? Did they have no idea that Cyrus was the murderer of Mr. Thatcher?

Cyrus rose. "Dieter?" he said. "Please go find the dog. Take the snowmobile – he's probably in the woods."

"Now?" said Dieter. "But—" Cyrus's eye patch twitched a little, as though there'd been a slight throb beneath it. "On my way," said Dieter. He left the room, putting on his coat.

"And Mrs. Meinhof?" Cyrus said. "Secure our guest in some quiet spot."

"Quiet spot?" said Mrs. Meinhof.

"Where I can continue our conversation while you prepare something nice and hot to drink."

"The basement storage room?"

"Perfect," Cyrus said.

"Now," said Mrs. Meinhof, tying the free end of the rope to an overhead pipe in the basement storage room, "we will see what is what."

Ingrid stood before her, wrists tied together tight, and said nothing. Mrs. Meinhof reached forward with one of those long-fingered hands and pinched her cheek, hard. Ingrid did her best not to cry, but her eyes filled with tears anyway. Mrs. Meinhof saw that and smiled.

"All set, Major," she called.

She left the room, went upstairs. Ingrid tried to

wriggle her wrists free. Not a chance: tied so tight her hands were swelling up. She tugged at the rope with all her strength, thinking maybe she could tear the pipe from the wall or at least bend it or something, but no. She gnawed at the rope with her teeth: useless.

Ingrid glanced around. Was there anything in the storage room that might help? Along one side stood shelves loaded with paint cans, plastic gasoline containers, bags of fertilizer, empty flower trays. Gardening tools – rakes, weed whackers, shovels, a chain saw – and a few card table chairs hung on the back wall. More shelves on the other side, loaded with sports equipment: croquet mallets, badminton racquets, fishing rods, tackle boxes. Lots of things that might be useful, if only they were a little closer.

She smelled smoke, glanced down. A weak and tiny plume of smoke, almost invisible, rose from the broken remains of the oil lamp, practically at her feet. What was that little cloth thing called, the part that actually caught fire? The wick? Yes. The chimney of the lamp was shattered, and so was the glass bottom that held the oil, but the wick in its metal ring was intact, the tail lying in a small glistening puddle. And there, against the wall, maybe in reaching distance of her right toe, lay a pile of old newspapers. What if—

Cyrus Ferrand walked through the doorway, a steaming mug in one hand, the murder weapon in the other. He took a sip, said, "Ah," set the mug on a shelf, unfolded a card table chair, and sat down, the rifle in his lap. "So," he said, "your grandfather taught you how to shoot. What else has he taught you?"

"I don't know what you mean," Ingrid said.

"Did you know he was quite the marksman?" said Cyrus. "But why am I speaking in the past tense? He hasn't lost his touch, it seems."

"Grampy didn't—"

"Go on," said Cyrus.

Ingrid was silent.

"Grampy didn't what?"

Ingrid kept her mouth shut.

"Didn't kill the conservation agent – is that what you were going to say?"

"I came for my dog," Ingrid said. "You can't keep me here over a dog."

Cyrus nodded. "A very sensible position. If only I were sure this rather minor crime was merely about a dog, you'd be home by now. Safe and sound."

Therefore she had to make him sure of that. "It is," she said. "I love Nigel."

Cyrus's voice rose, sharp and sudden. "Fritz. I named him myself."

"But no one here loves him," Ingrid said.

"How is that relevant? Mrs. Meinhof bought him – she has the receipt."

Ingrid remembered that moment on the village green, Mr. Samuels taking pictures for the World War II veterans story, when Cyrus had cast a long look at Nigel, probing and inquisitive. "Why didn't you say something instead of just taking him?"

"Negotiate with you?" said Cyrus. "Talk it out? Funny notion." He took the clippings from his pocket. "Let's return to your theft of these articles. What's your interest in them?"

"I told you," Ingrid said. "They're about my—"

His voice rose over hers, high and almost out of control in a moment, with no warning. "I don't have time for your games."

"I'm not—"

He rose suddenly, the rifle falling to the floor, and came toward her, thrusting the clippings in her face. "What does this mean to you?" He jabbed a finger, twisted and yellow nailed, at the margin: *DAMN IT TO HELL!* And at those two question marks and the three exclamation marks. Jab, jab. "What does it mean? What does it mean?"

"I don't know."

He raised his hand as though to smack her face. It trembled there, inches away. Then he lowered it. His eye shifted, tugged by some thought. He backed off. "You're a child, of course. Children can't be expected to understand. I'm sorry."

"Understand what?" Ingrid said. "About owning dogs, you mean?"

"Ingrid," he said. "Is that your name?"

"Yes."

"Is this really about dogs, Ingrid?"

"I told you and told you."

"Too insistently, if anything." He turned to one of the shelves, shifted a paint can aside, felt behind it. "Has your grandfather told you much about the war?" he said, much more quietly now, his back to her.

"No," she said.

"Predictable, I suppose," said Cyrus. "I'm sure he

prefers to keep the errors of his past a secret, especially from his beloved granddaughter."

"Errors?" said Ingrid.

"His conduct," said Cyrus, still fishing around on the shelf, "his real, unvarnished conduct, was rather shameful, after all."

"Grampy? Shameful?"

"A long time ago, of course, and one always hesitates to use a certain word, but I'm afraid it applies in his case."

"What word?" Ingrid said.

Cyrus smiled a rueful smile, like she was forcing him to act against his good breeding. "Coward," he said.

Ingrid's voice rose, shaking with rage, beyond any chance of control. "Grampy a coward? You're the coward. You stole Grampy's gun and ran away. You killed the fishermen. And it was all your fault in the first place, staying up on that ridge."

Cyrus turned to her, a small box in his hand. His voice was steady, even soft, but his face was getting redder and redder, an enormous blush that spread to the tips of his ears and down his neck, vanishing under his collar but reappearing again in his hands.

"So," he said, "not really about dogs after all."

Ingrid glared at him, said nothing. But way too late for silence. How could she have been this stupid, letting herself get trapped so easily? She thought again of that time on the village green, when Cyrus took that piercing look at Nigel. Something else had happened right after that, something, she was beginning to see, that turned out to be even more important. Mr. Samuels had said that Grampy had agreed to talk about his wartime exploits after so many years of silence, and had even promised a bombshell – his very word, according to Mr. Samuels, who seemed pretty excited about the whole thing. Not Cyrus's reaction: he'd gone pale and trembling. Now she knew why.

"You meant to kill Grampy, not Mr. Thatcher," she said. "To stop him from telling Mr. Samuels the truth about you."

Cyrus's mouth opened and closed. He turned even redder. "Lies on top of lies. And why did he want to spread them now, after so long?"

"If they were lies, you wouldn't be doing this," Ingrid said. She knew what had changed Grampy's mind, had discovered the answer at New York City Mercy Hospital, an answer she would keep to herself. Going silently to his grave would mean that this little bit of history – war history but also Echo Falls history – would have been forever false. Plus Grampy hated the Ferrands: that had to be part of it too.

Cyrus's good eye was on her, narrowing to almost nothing. The small box shook in his hand, made rattling sounds. Ingrid realized she'd seen boxes like that before, out at the farm. Cyrus opened it and took out some shells: .30-06. He started loading them into the magazine of the sniper gun. The action seemed to calm him, the redness fading from his skin. "All in all, this worked out just as well," he said, almost to himself. "Gave him something else to think about." His eye patch did that pulsing thing again. "And who believes a jailbird?" He started to close the magazine. Footsteps sounded on the stairs. Mrs. Meinhof entered.

"There's a man at the door," she said.

Cyrus turned to her in annoyance. "What man?"

"Can't place him, but I think I've seen him before," Mrs. Meinhof said.

"What help is that?" Cyrus's eye darted around. Down inside he was weak, Ingrid saw, and not good at making decisions, as he'd proved in Bataan. Up above someone pounded hard on the back door.

"I'd better have a look," Cyrus said. He left the storage room, rifle in hand.

"Wait," Mrs. Meinhof said. She took a rag from one of the shelves, ripped off a strip, and gagged Ingrid – her squirming did no good – tying it extra tight at the back. "There," she said. She followed Cyrus out of the storage room and up the stairs. Someone pounded on the door, harder this time.

Ingrid heard the back door open. Then came a man's voice. She couldn't make out what he was saying, but she knew that voice, knew it beyond doubt: Dad. Dad? She remembered calling into Ty's room that she was going to Chloe's, and later, when the Ferrands had driven her home, seeing the TT in the driveway. Ingrid tried to yell, tried to scream, succeeded only in making not-very-loud noises in her throat. She tugged on the rope, jerked at it with all her might: useless. At that moment she smelled smoke again, the smoke from the not-quite-extinguished oil lamp wick.

Ingrid reached out with her right leg toward that pile of old newspapers by the wall. Her leg was an inch too short. She stretched it out as far as she could, tried and tried. No good. What if she launched herself in the air, spun around – would that narrow the distance? Ingrid bent her knees as much as the rope would allow – not much – and jumped, at the same time spinning so her back faced the wall. She stuck out her foot. Her toe dragged on the edge of the top newspaper. Then the rope snapped her back down, almost tearing her arms out of their sockets. But: a whole newspaper now lay right in that oily puddle beside the smoking wick.

With her foot Ingrid nudged a corner of the newspaper so it just touched the wick. At first nothing happened. She listened, heard Cyrus say, "Perhaps she went on the ski trip," and Dad's reply, the words unclear, but she could tell he was raising some objection.

Burn, burn, burn.

"I assure you," Cyrus was saying, "if we hear anything at all..." Now Dad's reply was quieter, no longer argumentative. Ingrid made more of those throat noises. *Dad, Dad.* He couldn't hear, was about to go away, leave her behind in this basement, abandoned with terrible people. She screamed, "Dad! Dad!" but the sound got all muffled behind the gag. Ingrid screamed and screamed that muffled scream anyway, for a few moments unaware that down at her feet the little corner of newspaper was turning yellow. But then she noticed, in time to see a tiny flame appear, start to spread, half inch by half inch, finally meeting a patch of newspaper that was dampened with oil, probably kerosene in fact, like gasoline only—

"'Bye now," said Cyrus. "Nice seeing you." The door closed. *Dad! Dad!* And he was gone. But then came a *throompf*. With a sound like that – *throompf* – a real fire sprang up, waist height almost at once. So hot already, but there was no Plan B. The longer she waited, the harder it would get.

Ingrid raised up her bound wrists and held them to the flames.

twenty-six

ingrid tried to be precise, tried to keep the rope exactly right over the tip of the flame, to keep the fire off her skin, but it couldn't be done, at least by her. The flame wouldn't stay still, wanted to dance around, lick at the rope for a second or two and then jump suddenly at her wrists or hands, searing little jumps from which she jerked away, couldn't help herself. *Be brave, Griddie, suck it up.* Didn't real bravery start with just making a little effort to control fear? But it hurt so much, and besides, the fire was growing now, rising higher, burning hotter. In fact the whole pile of newspapers was smoking, and the rag that Mrs. Meinhof had torn a strip from looked about to—

Burst into flames. They spread almost at once to the bank of shelves to her right – the shelves with all those paint cans and plastic gasoline containers. The fire began making a noise, like the wind gathering strength, but not so loud that Ingrid didn't hear footsteps coming down the stairs.

Now, Griddie. Or never.

She held her wrists over the flame and kept them there. It felt like a long, long time, the strands of rope going through stages – blackening, smoking, sparking – before they caught fire and frayed apart, but it couldn't have been, because Mrs. Meinhof was just coming into the storage room when Ingrid twisted her hands free.

Mrs. Meinhof's eyes widened. "Wicked child! Major! Major!" She charged toward Ingrid, hands outstretched. Ingrid darted behind the flames, which now reached to the ceiling. Mrs. Meinhof glanced around wildly, looking for something to fight the fire with, saw nothing. She tore off her jacket and flapped it at the fire, a useless gesture, and worse than useless, because in seconds the jacket, too, went up in flames. And then, like fiery birds, flame balls flew into her wild hair, framing her face in a halo of fire. Mrs. Meinhof screamed. Something on the paint can shelf went *boom*. The whole room – and Mrs. Meinhof, too – was on fire, raging and beyond control. Ingrid ran out, a hot roaring at her heels.

She raced upstairs – no one around, not the slightest sign of what was happening down below – and headed along the hall toward the back door. It opened just as she reached for the knob.

Dieter walked in. "Couldn't find that stupid – hey! What the—?" She tried to dodge past him. He blocked her way, kicked the door shut behind him. "Major!"

Ingrid backed up, toward the living room. Behind her, Cyrus said, "What now?"

Ingrid wheeled around. Cyrus came out of the

living room, the Springfield in his hand. He saw her. His eye patch pulsed. "What's going on? Where's your mother?"

"Don't know," Dieter said. He sniffed the air. "Do you smell smoke?"

"No," said Cyrus. "Get her secured at once."

Dieter moved in on Ingrid from one end of the hall, Cyrus from the other. Ingrid ducked into the kitchen; nowhere else to go. They followed her. She ran behind the table like a character being chased in some stupid comedy. Dieter and Cyrus closed in from opposite sides, Dieter arriving first. Ingrid was trapped. Dieter's eyes shifted. He sniffed the air again.

"What are you waiting for?" Cyrus said. "Grab her."

Dieter reached out, caught her by the sleeve. At that moment a *boom* came from below, this one tremendous, and flames shot up through the floor, right where Dieter stood. The boards gave way with a splintering crack. Dieter lost his grip on her and fell through, down into the inferno, cut off in mid scream. Cyrus's mouth started to open. Ingrid dove under the table, scrambled toward the door. From the corner of her eye she saw the gun barrel rising. She launched herself into the hall. The rifle cracked behind her, and plaster exploded off the wall inches from her head. She ran down the hall, threw open the back door – the knob felt hot – and leaped outside.

The snowmobile stood in the yard. Ingrid had never even ridden on a snowmobile, had no clue how to drive one. She took a few steps toward the lane but stopped almost at once – headlights shone from that direction, coming her way. Ingrid crouched down, crossed the yard, hid behind a tree.

A car drove up the lane, parked at the edge of the yard. *Something about the shape of that car...* The driver's door opened and someone – a man – got out. *Something about the shape of that man...*

"Dad?"

"Ingrid?"

Then she was running, arms outstretched. He opened his own arms – hands white as snow in the moonlight – and wrapped them around her.

"Oh, Dad."

"What's going on?" Dad said. "I was driving away and Nigel came barking out of the woods, right in front of the car."

"You've got him?"

Dad pointed to the passenger seat, where Nigel—

Boom! This one the biggest of all. Flames boiled through the walls and roof of The Cottage, the noise, like a wild storm, so loud that Ingrid didn't hear the snowmobile until it was almost too late.

The snowmobile roared across the yard, Cyrus driving with one hand, the moonlight shining on the rifle in his other. The machine bore straight down, its single headlight exposing them clearly in the night. Dad had his back to the whole scene.

"Dad!"

Dad turned, saw the snowmobile, almost on them. He gave Ingrid a huge push, sent her flying. Then with a sickening crunch the snowmobile mowed him down.

The rifle pinwheeled away into the night. Dad lay still in the snow.

Ingrid ran to him, fell on her knees. He lay on his back, eyes closed. "Dad! Dad!" She took his head in her hands. His mouth opened. Blood trickled out one side, black in the moonlight. He spoke one word, hard to make out with his voice so thick: "Run." Ingrid looked up, saw the snowmobile veering in a tight turn, Cyrus hunched over the controls, coming back. She ran.

But where? Ingrid headed for the lane. If she could only get out of the woods, past the Ferrands' house, she might find help on the main road. But almost at once the snowmobile changed direction, cutting her off. She went the other way, past The Cottage, now blazing from top to bottom, a riot of red and orange flames, and into the trees.

Ingrid ran. Cyrus followed. The woods, so dense, protected her, forcing the snowmobile to slow down, slaloming through the trees. But there was nowhere to hide – that headlight kept finding her, throwing her running shadow across the snow. And then, all at once, there were no more trees. She was out of the woods, on a bare, steep slope down to the river.

No good. Ingrid cut to the right. Cyrus followed, was on her almost at once. *Roar.* A hand grabbed at her from the side. Ingrid fell. *Rip* – and her jacket was gone. Before she could get up, the snowmobile was bearing down, engine shrieking, and Cyrus shrieking something too, his mouth a round black hole. And then it was on her, looming huge. Ingrid rolled away, one snowmobile runner clipping her side, knocking the wind out of her.

The slope took over and rolled her, down, down and into the river.

But not into. The river was frozen, of course, and she landed hard on the ice, ice swept bare by the wind. She rose. The snowmobile barreled down the slope, relentless. Ingrid turned toward the river. Was it safe? Chief Strade had said the ice on the Punch Bowl was safe, and it had been, but she no longer trusted him. Was there a choice? Ingrid started running across the ice. It held.

The snowmobile howled after her, and Cyrus howled too. Ingrid ran with all her might, her whole being devoted to speed and only speed. But the ice was slippery and she wasn't a machine. The machine caught up fast, her shadow growing and growing in its headlight beam. At the last second she darted to one side – more of a lurch – and the snowmobile tore past.

Ingrid lost her balance, fell to the ice, hitting her head. She was stunned for a moment, and in that moment Cyrus swung around sharply and opened the throttle wide, hunched forward, coming fast. Ingrid started to rise, but oh so slow. And now there was no distance between them at all. His teeth were bared like a knife blade, and his eye patch flapped up in the wind. She was getting her feet under her – dizzy and oh so slow, the noise unbearable, the snowmobile filling her vision – when suddenly there came an enormous *crack*.

Crack!

And the snowmobile stopped dead. The engine snarled, but the machine went nowhere. Then it tilted, nose rising and rising, like the Titanic but much quicker, until the headlight pointed straight up at the sky. A second later the engine went silent and the headlight dimmed and flickered out. Cyrus's face registered a few quick expressions: disbelief, anger, terror. And maybe there would have been more, but he was out of time. The river made a soft sucking sound, and Cyrus and the snowmobile sank from sight in an instant, as though yanked down by some force on the bottom.

Ingrid crawled toward the hole in the ice, halted a few feet from the edge. A big bubble rose to the surface of the black water. Then came a few smaller bubbles and a single tiny one, bursting with a moonlit pop. After that, nothing.

Ingrid spotted something lying on the ice, close by: Cyrus Ferrand's eye patch. She didn't touch it.

Sirens sounded in the night, lots of sirens, getting louder. Ingrid turned toward the shore. The fire rose high, towering over the woods. Some of the trees were burning too, an enormous conflagration, but too distant to hear. The only sound now was a crackling, soft and quiet, almost inaudible: the hole freezing back up.

Ingrid spent the rest of that night and most of the next day in the hospital. Dad, with a broken pelvis, was there much longer. Mom took to visiting. Mrs. McGreevy got the asking price on her house almost at once and moved to Boston. Mom and Dad did a lot of talking in Dad's hospital room. Was he going to come back home? No one said, but Ingrid got the feeling that he wanted to and that Mom was still making up her mind. Mom was eating better now, had lost that hollowed-out look.

The ballistics tests cleared Grampy. The next day the Ferrand Group put out a press release saying Cyrus Ferrand had no connection to the group and that his actions, including the employment of the late private investigator Dieter Meinhof – and *his* actions, including but not limited to any possible trespassing on private property or anonymous calling to any state or local agencies – had taken place without the knowledge or approval of the Ferrand Group or the Ferrand family, who, individually and collectively, were gratified that justice was done. Dad got a small raise.

Ingrid helped Grampy move back to the farm. They chopped some wood – just Grampy, actually, Ingrid's hands not being quite up to it yet – and Grampy looked like his old strong self, split logs flying all over the place. Did that mean maybe he was somehow getting better? Ingrid had heard of things like that.

"Grampy?"

"Yup."

"How are you feeling?"

He paused, ax raised, and said, "What kind of question is that?"

"I just—"

"Tip-top," said Grampy.

And that was that.

Except that when Mom came to pick her up – Ingrid on her way out the door – Grampy put his hand on her shoulder and said, "You're in my will. Want you to know that."

"Oh, Grampy, I don't—"

"Guess what it is."

"What what is?"

"What I'm giving you."

"I don't want anything."

"Someone has to take care of the damn thing. Might be worth money someday."

"The Medal of Honor, Grampy? Oh, no, not me."

"Who's a better candidate?"

"Lots of people," Ingrid said. "And besides, I would never sell it."

"Proves the point," said Grampy. "Case closed."

"Grampy?"

"I said case closed."

"This is something else."

"Such as?"

"Such as if you ever go on a road trip, maybe I could come along."

"What kind of road trip?"

"Like New York."

Grampy's eyes narrowed.

"For example," Ingrid added quickly.

He gave her a long look.

Ingrid's hands were fine by opening night of *Hansel and Gretel* in Prescott Hall; just a few little scars here and there, nothing worth a second thought. After, backstage, the cast still in makeup, Brucie came over and said, "You scared the p—" Brucie saw his father approaching, changed the word he was about to say – "pants. You scared the pants off me."

"Huh?" said Ingrid.

"In the woods," Brucie said. "Your voice. How did

you make it so realis—"

But before he could finish his question, other people came swarming in, most of them surrounding Brucie, shaking his hand, patting him on the back. He'd brought down the house three or four times, come up with a funny ad-lib about bagel crumbs, and done a completely unrehearsed and dead-on imitation of Mick Jagger. His voice rose from the midst of all those fans. "Any studio execs in the crowd? Step right up."

Chief Strade and Joey approached.

"Stellar," said the chief.

"Thanks," said Ingrid. Their eyes met. Ingrid gave a little nod.

The chief turned to Joey. "Where's that bouquet?"

Joey patted his pockets. "Must have left it in the car."

But the bouquet – daisies – was still fairly fresh a few days later at the rec center dance. Joey handed Ingrid the flowers in the parking lot, minimizing the chance of any of the boys witnessing what could be interpreted as a romantic gesture.

"These are nice," Ingrid said. "Smell them."

Joey shook his head. They stood in silence, breath rising in the cold. Then Joey said, "I saw that movie. On DVD."

"What movie?"

"The one your mom likes."

"*Casablanca*?"

"Yeah." More silence. Joey shifted from one foot to the other, like he was building up to something. How long was this going to take? It was getting really cold.

"The funny thing is," he said at last, "you do kind of look like her."

Like Ingrid Bergman? "Don't be ridiculous," Ingrid said.

"You do," Joey said. "Especially, um, around the mouth."

He reached out and touched her lips with his finger, very gentle. A nice feeling – might even have been electric, if he hadn't had gloves on.

Welcome to Echo Falls.
Home of a thousand secrets.

Ingrid Levin-Hill – first-team soccer player, actress extraordinaire and unwilling detective – is in the wrong place at the wrong time. Or at least, her soccer boots are.

And getting them back without becoming a murder suspect means catching the killer herself. The police are on the wrong track and it's all Ingrid's fault. Like Alice in Wonderland, her life becomes curiouser and curiouser, turning Echo Falls into a nightmare. If only Ingrid could wake up...

**"One walloping good suspense yarn...
I couldn't put it down." Stephen King**

In Echo Falls,
everyone has a secret.

Too many things are amiss at 99 Maple Lane. What's bothering Ingrid's dad? Why has her brother Ty turned so moody? And when will everyone get off Grampy's back about selling his farm?

Meanwhile Ingrid stumbles upon some suspicious goings-on at the high school. Inspired by her hero, Sherlock Holmes, she begins fishing around to find out who's really pulling the strings in Echo Falls.

And then she gets kidnapped.

"I'm hooked on Echo Falls." Stephen King